THE DEAD WORLD OF LANTHORNE GHULES

THE DEAD WORLD OF LANTHORNE GHULES

Gerald Killingworth

Pushkin Children's

Pushkin Press
71–75 Shelton Street
London WC2H 9JQ

The Dead World of Lanthorne Ghules was first
published by Pushkin Press in 2019

1 3 5 7 9 8 6 4 2

ISBN 13: 978-1-78269-236-2

Designed and typeset by Tetragon, London
Printed and bound by CPI Group (UK) Ltd, Croydon, CRO 4YY

www.pushkinpress.com

THE DEAD WORLD
OF
LANTHORNE GHULES

House Hunting

A new baby! What was there to celebrate in that?

There were many other things twelve-year-old Edwin Robbins would much rather have celebrated—digging a swimming pool in the back garden, for instance. His parents had raised the subject of a pool quite often over the past year, and Edwin had already secretly drawn a plan of how one could be made to fit into the modest space available. He was going to invite his closest friends, Joe and Dom, round every day during the summer holidays, to splash about in it.

So much for promises and dreams.

"Of course, Edwin is thrilled to bits," his mother said with sickening regularity. "He almost jumped for joy when we broke the news to him."

How could she tell such lies? He hadn't smiled once since that black afternoon when they sat him down and told him that his longed-for little baby brother or sister was about to arrive in July—a whining, pooing, demanding creature that was far less fun than a pet.

THRILLED. *My armpits!* he wrote in giant letters in his diary. The "armpits" phrase was doing the rounds at school at the moment, and it seemed the only word which could begin to sum up his lack of enthusiasm for what was going to happen in three months' time.

Edwin's family celebrated the good news by visiting lots of relations, where the "thrilled to bits" lie was paraded around for everyone to admire. "You'll have to help look after the baby," said an aunt he now hated. His despair turned into a lump of lead in his stomach when all four grandparents told him he'd have to take a back seat and be a good brother. They never knew how close he was to shouting, "My Armpits!" at them. It wouldn't have done any good, so he just shrank into himself and planned how he could improve his tennis backhand.

At least he could take out his annoyance by hitting tennis balls as hard as possible at Joe and Dom. His parents had always wanted another child, he knew that, but they should have given up the idea when he was six or seven and not waited until he was a near-teenager.

Edwin tried to punish his father by saying, "You're nearly forty, Dad. I'm worried the baby's crying might send you deaf or round the bend."

Mr Robbins laughed. "Thanks for your concern, Edwin. I survived *your* constant howling, so I'm sure I'll be all right."

The visits and congratulations over "the wonderful news" eventually died down, and then there was the second bombshell. They were moving! It was, apparently, vital for this new intruder to have a bigger garden, and it couldn't grow up anywhere near a main road.

"I don't want to move," he told his parents.

"Don't be silly, Edwin. Of course we have to move. The traffic's dreadful these days."

"But I'm exactly the wrong age to change schools. I heard an expert say so on the TV."

"You'll still go to the same school. We won't be moving that far away. You'll just have to get up earlier, that's all."

"Like, about four o'clock in the morning," he replied sulkily.

Moving house was obviously as set in stone as the birth of the baby, but Mr and Mrs Robbins tried to make Edwin feel better about it by involving him in the choice of their new home.

One Saturday breakfast, Mrs Robbins said, "Dad's going to see some houses this afternoon, just to check the outsides and locations. If there's one that looks really promising, we'll all go and look at the inside next week. I need you to do the groundwork for me and take notes, there's a good boy."

Edwin and his father set off in the car sometime after two. It was a sultry afternoon, with a storm building, and the heaviness made Edwin irritable before they even drove away. He sat beside his father, with the pile of house details on his lap. Sweat ran down between his fingers and dampened the paper in the shape of his palm. This was swimming-pool weather, and they were going to have a baby instead. The sheer injustice of it made him silent and unresponsive, as his father chatted. But at least they agreed about the unsuitability of the first eleven houses they saw.

"Good thing Mum wasn't with us," said Mr Robbins. "She wouldn't have appreciated all these wastes of time. Shall we just cut our losses and go home, or is number twelve worth a try?"

Edwin knew his mother was hoping for good news on the house front. "Twelfth time lucky," he said. "It's called the Beanery and it's in Duck Pond Road. I'm surprised that didn't put Mum off. It says, 'Empty for the past year. Modernization required, but will repay sensitive attention.' What does that mean, Dad?"

"It's probably a ruin and the picture's a lie. But Mum was rather taken with the details, so let's give it a whirl."

Soon they were standing outside the Beanery, not knowing what to make of it. With two or three of its neighbours, it was probably all that was left of a village from before the town expanded beyond it. As no one currently lived there, Edwin and his father had no compunction about entering the wild garden and peering through the windows.

"I wonder," said Mr Robbins when they went around the back, "if... Yes, it is. That's lucky."

The padlock on the back door came away in his hand. Well, it gave, after he had twisted it for a bit, and, with no feelings of guilt at all, they went inside.

"I like what I see," said Mr Robbins as soon as they entered the kitchen, with its red-tiled floor and a chunky beam across the centre of the ceiling. "It has what they call 'potential', wouldn't you say? I can feel myself getting excited, Edwin, and that hasn't happened with any of the other houses."

They went round checking what they could see against their printed details. The floorplan turned out to be nowhere as neat as the details suggested, and Edwin had to admit that there was the possibility of fun in a house with two staircases and cupboards in unexpected places.

Mr Robbins paced up and down checking measurements, which Edwin had to write down in a notebook, and he looked all over for traces of rot and woodworm. From time to time he yelped. Edwin thought this was probably a dangerous sign. When Mr Robbins decided on a second tour, yelps still included, Edwin stayed behind in the brightest of the downstairs rooms, writing his own comments to show his mother later. No furniture had been left by the last owner, but Edwin found a comfortable seat on the broad stone hearth.

Leaning his back against the edge of the fireplace, which was made of three more blocks of the same stone, he settled his behind into a shallow dip and made a few inexpert drawings with arrows and labels. As he sat there sketching and writing, a slight fall of soot from the chimney made him start. He looked into the deep grate. It still contained the remains of the last fire lit there, some charred logs and a handful of sheets of paper. What could these sheets of paper tell him about the last owners, he wondered and dislodged one of them with his pen. It had printing on it and was probably no more than a year-old newspaper. Curiosity made him cast his eye over it, all the same, and it turned out to be a series of advertisements, or parts of advertisements, with the charring from the fire obliterating much of what had been written.

Has proved spectacularly useful in locating those who are suspected of being lost in the mists of time, he read.

What an odd thing to write.

Green scabs peel themselves off, apologize and vanish in minutes.

That was even odder. He couldn't make out the name of the product, but who on earth would need to buy it?

Then there were some "personals".

If you encounter my brother, please tell him that we have forgiven the fizzing warts.

Edwin laughed. He liked magazines like this, with spoof stories and joke advertisements. He turned to the corner of the page where you could read about *Pen Pals of every taste, shape and length of nose.*

I'd like a pen pal, he thought. *One I don't have to write to in French, though. That's too much like hard work.*

He set about finding a new imaginary friend, from the brief list that had not gone up in flames. One description in particular caught his eye:

Young creature just learning the ways and how to make up his own mind, seeks equally positive youngster not put off by other family members with revolting habits. They are of that kind, but I'm not allowed to say too much. If all you have to do in the evenings is listen to your own animated thoughts, then drop me a line. Replies may be placed in a convenient chimney and will be responded to unless they fall into the wrong hands. In which case, look out, because I can't be held responsible. Your new friend, perhaps,

L Ghules

Edwin chuckled and tore a sheet of paper from his notebook. On it, he wrote:

Dear L Ghules, My name is Edwin and I am twelve years old. I would have liked a swimming pool, but I am going to take delivery of a baby instead. My current best friends have stopped being sympathetic. It would be very nice to have a new friend when I have got fed up with being a slave. My parents think I am thrilled to bits, but little do they know. I could tell you what I really think, if you like, and you could do the same.

He folded the piece of paper and held it out over the remains of the fire, directly underneath the chimney, meaning to throw it away with the other rubbish. Before he could let go of it, there was a whooshing sound and a brief tug on his fingers. The smile on his face disappeared in an instant, as the piece of paper shot upwards, followed by the distinct sound of machinery—*click*, then *ping*.

Edwin jumped back, and felt absolutely no temptation to look up the chimney to see where the message had gone and why. His brain said it was an unusual air current, probably, but it also said *Get out of there, before anything worse happens*, and so that is what he did.

Well, events took their natural course after that.

The baby arrived on time and was called Mandoline. Edwin absolutely refused to say the name in anything but a mutter. Whatever had possessed his mother to call her longed-for second child after a musical instrument? And they didn't buy the Beanery. The "modernization required", they decided, was far too much trouble, so they settled for a larger house in Grindling Close, a new development a few miles away. It had the big garden his parents wanted and a large, open fireplace in the lounge, over which Mandoline was going to hang her first ever Christmas stocking.

One miserable Saturday morning early in November, Mr and Mrs Robbins took Mandoline out, to display her to a new set of friends. Edwin was allowed to stay at home to "get on with all my homework", as long as he didn't spend hours on his phone chatting to Joe and Dom. He sat by the fire, intermittently reading his history textbook and taking in very little about the Wars of the Roses. A sudden skittering sound made him jump.

A fall of soot had dislodged itself from the chimney and landed in a dark shower on the fire. Something else had fallen too; a tiny bundle that must have been travelling with the soot, hit the edge of the fender and bounced in the direction of Edwin's foot. He picked the object up and was astounded to see that it bore his name, written in the tiniest of crabbed scripts. *For Edwin,* it said and then, *Please read and reply in haste.*

He wiped off the traces of soot that were still clinging to the bundle and turned the object over several times. It was warm, and it also gave off a drainy pong which he couldn't flap away. He could have sworn that the lettering glowed—or throbbed, even—to gain his attention. Edwin's finger found a raised edge, and he was able to prise apart the two halves of what turned out to be an envelope containing a letter. Once it had been freed from its envelope, the single page letter grew until it was about six times its original size. Edwin was both horrified and fascinated. Part of him wanted to throw the weird piece of mail into the fire and the other part wanted to read it and discover who the writer was and how they had come by his name.

He read it, of course.

Dear Edwin,

Thank you so much for your letter. I am sorry it has taken this long for me to reply, but there has been a fault in the chimneys. The wrong sort of smoke, they say. Yours was easily the most interesting letter I received. I'm sorry you haven't got your pool. I could send you some newts if you like, but they might get burnt if they arrived when there was a fire. Do you like cooked newts? I never have.

I would like to write more but my horrible auntie is due to arrive for one of her visits and I have to find somewhere to hide. Please write soon. The smoke seems all right now.

Your pen-friend,

Lanthorne Ghules

It was then that Edwin threw the letter into the fire and ran out of the room. There was no way that he was EVER going to reply to such a peculiar letter. How could a moment's thoughtless fun go so horribly, horribly wrong?

2

Bumps in the Night

A couple of weeks later, Edwin was having a bad time at home. He was accused of being both uninterested in Mandoline and "sometimes not very nice". He even heard the J word used a couple of times—whispered, of course, but he caught it distinctly. J for jealousy. Edwin wasn't jealous; he felt misunderstood and left out. And now here he was, once again, being asked to "keep an eye on Mandoline" while his mother faffed about with something unimportant in the kitchen. His father rarely kept an eye on Mandoline at all. So much for being an adoring parent.

"You've got to promise me not to cry," Edwin told his sister, as soon as Mrs Robbins left the room. "Because I'll get the blame. You know that."

It was a rash thing to say. Mandoline narrowed her eyes and stared at Edwin. Her bottom lip trembled. She wasn't going to get him into trouble in the first minute, was she? Only five months old and already she was so cunning. He knew, he just knew, that when she learnt to speak, she would invent all sorts of untrue tales about him, and his parents would believe every word.

"Look at the funny bunny," he said.

The bright-yellow rabbit, with its overlong ears and jingly rattle, didn't amuse Mandoline at all. She settled into a persistent low-level grizzle, which Edwin felt pretty confident wasn't loud enough to reach the ears of his mother in the kitchen. He sat glumly on the floor, expecting time to pass agonizingly slowly until he was set free from this babysitting hell.

Then he suddenly felt a rush of air on his face, a warm but damp and smelly breath accompanied by a sound effect he was afraid he recognized. The logs on the fire flared dramatically as the strange air blew over them. A few sparks crackled, and the sound made Mandoline jump. She began to cry properly. Edwin knew he would need to soothe his sister before his mother rushed in and shouted at him, but, for a few moments, he wasn't able to move at all.

The whooshing air had brought with it something very unwelcome—another tiny letter. If he threw it onto the fire unread, Edwin was sure it would shoot back out again, and probably land on Mandoline and set her alight. So, snatching the little packet, he pushed it down into his pocket, where he could feel its warmth against his leg. Then he had to attend to Mandoline.

He leant over the carrycot and made meaningless noises at his sister, who began to wail in loud sobs fed by deep gasps for breath. She certainly knew how to give a performance. Edwin took hold of Mandoline's fingers and began the pat-a-cake game which generally amused her. Horror! A dusting of soot on the letter had transferred itself to his hands, and Mandoline's pink jacket now sported Edwin's black hand print.

Mrs Robbins emerged from the kitchen.

"Why is Mandoline crying? Edwin, you've covered her in soot!"

Panic made Edwin inventive. "The logs on the fire exploded. There were burning sparks everywhere. Mandoline was frightened and I thought the house might catch fire. I sorted out the fire and I got a bit dirty and she's all right. But there's a funny smell 'cause she might need changing."

It was a long excuse and his voice got louder and louder as he said it, but it worked.

"You've been a sensible boy," said Mrs Robbins.

"I'm going upstairs," Edwin told her. He felt he needed to do this quickly, in case the letter became impatient to be read and opened up and burst out of his pocket.

By the time he reached his room, the letter had cooled down—although his annoyance at receiving it hadn't. Some of the smell still lingered. As soon as Edwin broke the seal, the remaining soot on it blew off in a *poof!* and the letter expanded to reading size. There was a new and unexpected feature this time too, an unnerving one. As the letter opened, a voice came out of it. It sounded clear, if a little echoey.

"Hello, Edwin. This is Lanthorne. I can't say any more because it's too expen—" The message ended in a squeak.

At least he sounds like a boy, thought Edwin, *and not like a...* He couldn't finish the sentence, because it was all so peculiar and Lanthorne might be an octopus for all he knew. He wanted to bail out, to turn back time, but here he was with a second letter and a VOICE introducing it. Taking a deep breath, Edwin began to read.

Dear Edwin,

I was so looking forward to another letter from you. I expect it got caught in the soot. I know that can happen with communications from your side. So here I am, hiding in the cellar and writing down more of my thoughts. Your family sound as difficult as mine. I'm always in the wrong for wanting to find things out, but isn't that what young people are meant to do? My terrible Auntie Necra is visiting us again, and my parents never try to stop her when she goes on about... but you don't want to know about that. I hate this cellar. I hope we won't have to hide here when you visit. I've got a special friend who lets me use his chimney for my letters, and he gave me the money for the voiceover. Is your cellar big enough for both of us?

Please put a message up the chimney very, very soon.

Your best friend,   Lanthorne

Although a large part of Edwin—in fact, all of him—still wanted nothing at all to do with strange letters blowing out of chimneys, accompanied by the smell of drains, he sympathized with Lanthorne's comments about his difficult family. Here was someone he could talk to, even if it meant having their conversation by way of the chimney.

It's never a good idea to write a letter in haste, but Edwin needed to sound off.

Dear Lanthorne, he wrote.

I'm being kept prisoner in my bedroom. When my little baby sister, who was stupidly named after a musical instrument, learns to crawl, I expect she'll come in here all the time, and then I'll have to retreat into a cellar like you. Do you have a little baby sister too? Does she get you into trouble when she makes even the smallest sound? If you don't have one, please feel free to take mine. I'll even wrap her up for you. Let's meet for a burger, or whatever, and have a good moan about our parents.   Edwin

It was a short reply and Edwin wasn't happy with the way he ended; all the same, he marched defiantly downstairs and threw it up the chimney.

"What are you doing, Edwin?" asked his mother, who came into the room just as he was delivering the letter.

"I've written to Father Christmas, saying I don't want any presents this year. He's to give them all to Mandoline. That's what you and Dad want, isn't it?"

Mrs Robbins was taken aback. "There's no need for sarcasm, Edwin." She went to give him a hug, but Edwin stomped off. He was beyond hugs, at that moment.

Mr Robbins had obviously been told to have a word with his son during supper. He managed it very badly.

As they finished their lemon meringue pie, he said, "Mum tells me you're being difficult, Edwin." The J word was used twice.

"I didn't say that at all," said Mrs Robbins sharply.

"I'm thinking of running away," said Edwin. "Is it all right to leave the table to do that?"

He spent the evening fairly contentedly in his room, playing a computer game and writing rude comments about his parents and sister in his diary. That day's entry ran to two pages. His mother knocked on his door twice, once to ask if he wanted to watch a comedy programme on the television and the second time to say she had opened a tub of ice cream. Edwin was distant and negative each time. He felt he had the upper hand for once, and he was enjoying it.

Edwin had been in bed for about an hour when his parents came upstairs. He was amused to hear that they were still bickering about what had been said to him.

"You don't know the meaning of tact."

"*You* said talk to him. It wasn't necessary."

"He's going through a stage."

"So are you."

Their bedroom door shut loudly, and Edwin fell asleep to the distant buzz of their continuing argument. He woke up sometime after midnight, thinking, *They can't still be at it.* He could hear a tapping, whispering sort of noise. Perhaps his mother was knocking on his door, begging for forgiveness. Edwin sat up in bed and looked towards the bedroom door, but that wasn't where the noise was coming from.

The tapping and whispering hadn't stopped, and Edwin realized he could distinguish words, his name.

"Edwin, it's me, Lanthorne. Let me through."

Edwin was suddenly cold from head to foot. Around the edge of the door to his bedroom cupboard was a faint light, and behind it, Lanthorne Ghules was tapping, perhaps with claws or extra-long teeth. Edwin's temperature dropped another degree. The catch on the door was unreliable, and it sometimes swung open of its own accord. What if that happened now?

"Edwin, I know you're on the other side."

The light around the door didn't grow any brighter, but a smell was seeping into his bedroom now, a drainy smell like the one that clung to Lanthorne's letters. Edwin tried lying there with his fingers jammed into his ears and both pillows over his head, but each time he surfaced, the tapping and whispering was still going on. He felt invaded, cornered. Gathering an ounce of courage, he jumped out of bed and switched on his radio and computer. He found a music station on each of them and turned the volume up to maximum.

Very soon, Mr Robbins burst into the room and stood there glaring at Edwin.

"Edwin, what is going on?"

"I had a nightmare. Music frightens it away."

Little did his father know just how real the nightmare was, and how near. The bogeyman—the bogeyboy actually—really *was* hiding in the cupboard.

"Well, it's a shame about the nightmare, Edwin, but you can't keep the whole house awake." Mr Robbins gave several long sniffs and looked quizzical.

"I wouldn't want to disturb Mandoline," Edwin said pointedly.

"Keep your light on for a bit and play the radio quietly. That should do the trick." Mr Robbins sniffed again, thought about saying something more, decided not to, ruffled his son's hair, said, "See you in the morning" and left.

Edwin switched off his computer and sat on the edge of his bed, praying that the only sound he would hear would be that stupid song on the radio.

Prayers have a habit of not being answered.

Tap, tap. "Edwin, I'm still here."

"Armpits off!" Edwin growled. He wanted to run up and shout it through the crack in the cupboard door, but he remembered that if you trod on a certain part of the carpet in front of the door, it affected the loose catch. Also, if he started shouting, it would bring his father back.

The tapping and whispering finally stopped. After twenty minutes, Edwin turned off the bedroom light and saw that the light around the cupboard door had also gone. It might be a trick, of course. He turned his light to half brightness and opened the bedroom door a little way, in case he had to make his escape. Then he tried to get back to sleep, not an easy thing in the circumstances.

3

A Visitor

The next morning was Sunday and the Robbinses always took their time over a big breakfast. No one mentioned loud music in the night, and the J word didn't pop up once. Mandoline was fed and tidied and left to gurgle in a world of her own, while her family enjoyed their breakfast. Edwin noticed that he was given twice his normal serving of scrambled eggs.

"Look at those pigeons," said Mrs Robbins. "I gave them a plateful of scraps first thing and now they're practically banging on the window for more."

She got up from the table and shooed the birds away, but they were soon back.

"I was thinking Edwin could help me clean the garden furniture and put it in the shed for the winter," said Mr Robbins.

"Don't mind," said Edwin. He thought of adding, in his most cutting voice, *Why not ask Mandoline to do it? She is Superbaby, after all.* Instead, he poured himself the last of the orange juice.

Outside, on the patio, there was a round white table and a set of chairs, which they used for meals whenever it was warm enough. The furniture should have been put away two weeks ago, because there had been no Bonfire Night party in case the noise frightened Mandoline. Edwin was convinced Mandoline would have slept through the loudest bangers just to prove them wrong. He missed having their own fireworks party.

Edwin and his father wiped down and dried the table and chairs, while regularly having to shoo away the determined pigeons. Then the furniture needed to be folded up and stacked in the shed. Edwin didn't mind helping. It delayed the moment when he had to sit down with his maths homework. He had copied the answers from Dom, who was a maths genius, but he still had to make the working fit. Poor working and correct answers pointed to only one thing: cheating. Edwin had been caught out like that before.

Another reason he was happy to be outside was because it kept him away from the discussion about "feelings" that he sensed his mother wanted to have with him. He couldn't cope with feelings, on top of there being a weird boy in his bedroom cupboard. That was asking too much of anybody, surely?

"Work done," said Mr Robbins as they stacked the last of the chairs. "No thanks to those pigeons. What's got into them? Fancy a beer, Edwin?"

"Not just now, thanks. I'm driving."

They often shared this joke, although Edwin was beginning to think it was about time his father actually allowed him a taste of beer rather than just laughing about it.

Mr Robbins went inside, leaving Edwin alone in the garden. He mooched about, out of sight of the kitchen window, and took swipes at the dried heads which still lingered on a number of the flowers. He felt that events were closing in on him. True, no one had made him write that first letter and put it up the chimney in the Beanery, but it was a bit much to now have a strange boy trying to get out of his bedroom cupboard. He picked up a bedraggled tennis ball, which had got itself lost in the summer, and threw it half-heartedly at the pigeons.

One of the daft creatures must have sneaked into the shed when they were putting the garden furniture away. Edwin could hear it fluttering madly against the door. He had a good mind to let it stay there all day, but he wasn't a spiteful boy and so he sauntered over to the shed and pulled the door open. He was about to say, "Come out, you stupid bird", but the words died in his mouth. In front of him, stood a small, grey boy several inches shorter than himself, with his hands over his eyes and crying in pain.

"It's so bright! It's so bright!" the boy kept saying.

Edwin knew at once this was Lanthorne Ghules, and his first thoughts were ones of sheer relief—*He's only a boy, after all, He's shorter than I am* and *He doesn't have claws or fangs*!

There was real distress in Lanthorne's voice, so Edwin pushed him into the shed and banged the door shut behind them. Even in the gloomy interior, Lanthorne continued to stand with his hands over his eyes and seemed hardly aware of Edwin. He repeated, "It's so bright!" over and over again, as if there were no other words in his vocabulary. Edwin began to worry that Lanthorne had been blinded or lost his mind.

"If it hurts your eyes, try peeping through a couple of your fingers," Edwin suggested. Most of the shed's single window was covered by some lengths of wood standing on end, so he couldn't understand why Lanthorne was so uncomfortable.

Lanthorne said, "It's so bright" a few times more, then followed Edwin's advice. "I can see you," he said eventually.

Edwin was relieved. No blindness. Perhaps this story wasn't going to have a terrible ending.

Lanthorne peeped through a few more fingers, before finally taking his hands away altogether. "I'm Lanthorne."

"I know. And I'm Edwin."

"I know."

"Let's sit down," said Edwin.

He quickly unstacked two of the chairs, and they sat down opposite each other and stared. And stared. It wasn't a very big shed, so they really were almost eyeball to eyeball.

"Sorry about last night," Edwin said at last. He wasn't sure how truthful he could be. "I thought you might be a werewolf or an arachnid. You know, dangerous. Bloodsucking. Fangs." He hoped that Lanthorne would laugh at this description of himself, but there wasn't even the beginning of a smile.

"Is everything here on fire?" Lanthorne asked. He moved his chair so that he now had his back to the window. Edwin didn't switch on the light.

The conversation lapsed into more staring. Edwin wondered how rude it would sound if he pointed out how grey Lanthorne was. It wasn't just that the shed was gloomy; Lanthorne really was a pale grey colour. Not dirty, but a genuine puddle-water grey. He had all the features of a normal, if small, boy—untidy, spiky hair; eyes, nose, ears and mouth in the correct places; arms and legs the length you would expect; ten fingers—but grey skin. His hair was grey too, and his eyes, Edwin noticed uneasily, had hardly any colour at all.

Edwin was fairly sure Lanthorne was wearing a jumper and shorts, but his clothes were so shapeless and so dark they made him look like a charcoal smudge with a head and limbs attached to it. In the stuffiness of the shed, Edwin was also aware of something else—a whiff of drains.

"Excuse me, but you're very big," said Lanthorne.

"Am I?" replied Edwin, who knew he wasn't. Everything about Lanthorne was dainty, pinched, as if he had left part of himself behind.

"And you're shinier than I expected. We call you people 'Shiners'. Your hair looks as if it's going to catch fire."

"My hair's dark brown. Pretty dull, when you think about it."

Edwin's hair wasn't glossy chestnut or ginger, and yet Lanthorne called it shiny. No wonder his visitor couldn't take the light outside.

"I thought I was going blind. Have you got special eyes?"

"Not really," said Edwin. "Mum says I might need glasses eventually."

There followed more staring and a lot of awkward fidgeting. Lanthorne looked more and more uncomfortable, as if he was sorry for finding a way into Edwin's world. Edwin still hadn't asked his two big questions, and now they both burst out of him.

"Where do you come from? And how did you get here?"

"I'm ever so thirsty," said Lanthorne. "Coming through has sort of dried me out. My friend said it might."

"I'll go into the house and fetch you something."

It was frustrating not to have answers to these giant questions, but Edwin was glad to go out into the fresh air again. There was a staleness about Lanthorne, a lack of freshness which wasn't exactly what Edwin's mother called "high", but he wasn't the sort of person you wanted to sit close to in an enclosed space for any length of time.

"Stay here quietly while I get us a drink and a snack. Try not to be seen, okay?"

Lanthorne hunched down and clutched the edges of his chair. Edwin noticed how spindly his arms were.

"What will your people do to me if they know I'm here?"

"They won't lock you in the cellar," Edwin laughed. This was another joke that fell very flat on its face.

"Shall I hide under something?"

"Just don't peep out of the window. My mum and dad are the sort who think it's all right to ask lots of questions if friends come round. They don't realize it drives people away."

33

"I think I'll hide in that corner, anyway. It's like our cellar at home, and I can curl up so you won't notice I'm there."

When Edwin returned to the shed, he honestly hoped he would find it empty. He'd had enough of this adventure already. Once he was inside again and the door was closed, a grey head appeared from behind the pile of boxes in the corner.

"Told you," said Lanthorne. "It was just like home, but a bit more comfortable."

"I've got biscuits and lemonade," said Edwin. He handed Lanthorne one of the chilled cans of drink and tore open the packets of biscuits.

"Lovely and cold," said Lanthorne, wrapping his thin fingers around the can with some difficulty. He then tried to bite it.

"You open it like this."

Edwin tugged the ring pull and a spray of lemon-scented bubbles escaped. Lanthorne was enchanted.

"Now what do I do?"

Edwin drank from his own can, to show Lanthorne how it was done. After the first mouthful, Lanthorne's eyes were wide with delight.

"It's all sweet and tingly," he said and gulped down several more mouthfuls so quickly he couldn't hold back a loud burp.

"I've got some Iced Moments biscuits, and we call

these 'squashed-fly' ones as a joke because of the black bits."

"I want those," said Lanthorne and grabbed a strip of the garibaldi biscuits.

"They're currants, actually, not flies," Edwin pointed out.

Did Lanthorne really look disappointed on hearing this? Edwin hoped he was wrong.

They settled themselves on their chairs. "I want to know all about you," said Edwin. To himself, silently, he added, *And please don't tell me you're a ghost or a vampire.* He noted some pieces of wood in the corner, which could serve as a makeshift cross or stake in case Lanthorne turned out to be either of these horrors.

"I live in Landarn. It's a bit different from here. Not many of us believe in you Shiners, but my friend has told me stories about you ever since I was little. Some of the stories say you catch fire and burn up as soon as we touch you."

"That's ridiculous."

Lanthorne leant across and gave Edwin a delicate pinch. "There! I knew it wasn't true," he said. "Can I try those other ones?"

Edwin handed over the entire packet of Iced Moments.

"My friend says our two worlds are sort of back-to-back and if you look very carefully you can open doors between them. I needed his help to find this door, but I mustn't stay long."

That's a relief, thought Edwin. Lanthorne was going to have to leave soon, like Cinderella at the ball.

"The problem is you can't just go through a door when you feel like it. They're funny things, with a will of their own."

At least that meant people in Edwin's world were safe from grey people popping out every time they opened a cupboard!

"Who is this friend of yours?" Edwin asked.

"He's wise and he's read lots of old books, so he knows all about Shiners. He says you can't live very long because the fire inside you burns you up. Sorry, it was a bit unkind to mention that."

"Tell your friend he's wrong. We live for ages. I've got a great-grandmother who's eighty-five."

"I'll pass on the information to my friend. He likes to get things right. It's time I was getting back. But don't worry, I'll stay for hours next time."

"How will you get home?" There was panic in Edwin's voice.

"My friend said I'd be able to use the same door, if I didn't stay very long."

"You mean the door of this shed?"

"Yes. I need to go outside, and when I come back in I'll be home."

"If I try to enter the shed later this afternoon, will I walk straight into your world as well?" There was no way Edwin wanted that.

"No. That can't happen. The door only opened for me. But, Edwin, I'm afraid to go into the light again."

Edwin needed to think clearly. He couldn't have a boy from another world setting up home in his shed for ever. "Put your jumper over your head to protect your eyes, and I'll guide you to the door handle," he said.

"I think you're even wiser than my other friend, Edwin."

No, I'm not, thought Edwin. *I just want this to be over.* "Put the biscuits in your pocket," he suggested, and he had to turn away when Lanthorne took off his jumper because a lot more of the stale smell was set free.

Hoping that his parents were nowhere near, Edwin took Lanthorne by the arm and led him out of the shed. Then he turned Lanthorne round and placed the grey boy's fingers on the door handle. He was surprised how distinctly cool Lanthorne's skin felt.

"Quickly, before my parents see you."

"I've had a lovely time, Edwin. Thank you."

Lanthorne opened the shed door and stepped through. An intense smell of drains wafted over Edwin, who slammed the door shut, hoping he hadn't sent Lanthorne flying as he did so.

"Who was that boy?" asked Mrs Robbins as Edwin hurried into the house.

Yet again, Edwin had to come up with a story instantly.

"He's new at school."

"Why did he have his jumper over his head?" Mrs Robbins didn't miss much.

"We're starting a secret society. You shouldn't be watching. That was our special sign, and now we'll have to think of another one."

"He isn't still in the shed, is he?"

"No. He had to get home... I think I can hear Mandoline crying."

"Have a quick look at her for me, will you?"

"I'm too dirty. I might leave a black handprint on her."

Edwin was annoyed that his mother had spotted Lanthorne. At least she hadn't noticed how grey he was. She would make an excellent spy, watching people's every move and then asking questions that threw them off balance. He would need to be as careful as possible if Lanthorne tried to visit him again. *Please let him not find another door.*

Later that afternoon as it was getting dark, Edwin revisited the shed. His parents were watching an antiques programme on the television, and he was sure his movements weren't followed. He dreaded finding Lanthorne still in the shed and, even more, he dreaded opening the door and walking into Lanthorne's smelly world. Gingerly, inch by inch, he pulled the shed door open and peeped through the crack. It was still their shed and there was no grey boy hiding inside.

Phew! That's all over and done with, Edwin thought. But of course it wasn't.

4

What Am I Doing Here?

The Christmas holidays came. Edwin always spent the first day of every school holiday as lazily as he could, just to make the point that lessons were over. He didn't even bother to call Joe or Dom. He came downstairs for a late breakfast—three bowls of cereal and more orange juice than was comfortable—then went straight back to his room, where he turned on the radio (not too loud to disturb Mandoline, naturally) and got back under the duvet. The best part of this lazy day was that he could lie there wearing only T shirt, underpants and socks, and doze and think about nothing in particular. His time was completely his own. Unusually, he skipped lunch because he was too comfortable to get out of bed.

At half past two, his mother knocked and called softly, "You're not feeling unhappy are you, Edwin?"

"No, Mum. I'm relaxing and deciding what to buy people for Christmas."

He'd really been trying to work out how much he could persuade his parents and grandparents to buy *him*, but there was the other side of the coin to think about as well. He amused himself dreaming up joke presents. Mandoline was queen of their family and would probably go on to rule the world, so he could buy her a brightly coloured plastic crown, with huge jewels set in it. For his mother, a pair of boxing gloves, because she kept "having words" with the neighbours whose cat was using the Robbinses' garden as its litter tray. His father was planning some very ambitious DIY, and Edwin thought he needed a swear box for when it all fell apart—a china pig or Tardis money-box that gave you chocolate buttons every time you inserted a coin. A swear box would soon fill up, if past DIY disasters were anything to go by.

Mrs Robbins knocked on the bedroom door again a little later, and this time she came in. Edwin put on his most smiley face and pretended he was singing along to the song playing on the radio. On the first day of the holiday, he wasn't prepared to have an "Are you sure you're not unhappy?" conversation. His mother put six five-pound notes on his bedside table and turned down the radio.

"This is to help with your Christmas shopping. I don't believe Santa takes plastic."

Edwin was thrilled. He'd been saving up for presents for two months, but an extra thirty pounds was perfect! Once his mother left, he got out of bed and looked over to the cupboard where he kept his cash box hidden.

It was a rather obvious place to hide his special possessions, but modern houses don't go in for spaces under loose floorboards or behind removable bricks, where you can secrete things you don't want other people to see. The cash box was an inspired present, last Christmas, from his grandparents. It looked like a treasure chest and had a huge key. He kept it at the bottom of a holdall packed with archaeology magazines, while its key was sellotaped to the underside of the lowest shelf in the cupboard. Looking at the cupboard door brought Lanthorne Ghules to mind, naturally, but Edwin had opened the door loads of times in the weeks since Lanthorne's frantic banging from the other side, so the sight of it no longer caused him even the slightest shiver.

His mind full of what he could now afford to buy with this extra money, Edwin opened the cupboard door quite casually. As he started to bend down towards the holdall with the cash box, he felt himself propelled violently forwards. There was barely time for him to cry out in surprise as he passed straight into the dead, grey world of Lanthorne Ghules, which he'd hoped he would never see.

It felt as if he had walked into an explosion, not the kind that hurls you backwards for hundreds of feet, but the sort that, like the flat of an enormous hand, smacks every part of you very hard, from your forehead down to your ankles. He rocked backwards and then pitched forwards onto his knees, so shocked by what had happened he could hardly breathe. There was much less light now and the air all around him was clingy in a damp, unpleasant way. He didn't want to take it down into his lungs. Eventually he was forced to, and his gasp was so powerful it hurt his windpipe.

A small hand touched his shoulder. "Hello, Edwin. Are you all right?"

Edwin was in no way all right. He had just crossed over into a badly lit, smelly room in another world, *in his underpants*. Not being all right couldn't get much worse than this. He struggled to his feet and glared at Lanthorne, who was obviously thrilled to have this unexpected visitor in his bedroom. As much as a grey face and dull teeth can manage it, he beamed.

"Send me home, right away," Edwin said angrily. He embarrassed himself by stamping his foot. "You shouldn't have brought me here."

"I didn't bring you here. And the connecting door-way's gone."

There was only one word Edwin knew which could express his outrage at the situation he found himself in. As he prepared to yell it at the absolute top of his voice, Lanthorne's delicate but strong hand stifled him.

"You mustn't let anyone hear you. It isn't safe."

"What will they do? Eat me?" Edwin snapped.

Lanthorne's strange expression made Edwin regret his question immediately. His legs wobbled and he allowed himself to be led across the room to Lanthorne's bed, where he could sit down.

For a few moments, Edwin sat with his head in his hands, refusing to look around him or to take notice of Lanthorne repeatedly tapping him on the arm and speaking his name. He felt as if all the worst moments in his life—every terror, every disappointment—had been rolled into a hard ball which was being banged up and down on his head by someone extremely nasty. At last, he opened his eyes and brushed away Lanthorne's hand. If he inhaled in shallow breaths, the "off" smell wasn't so bad, which meant he was growing used to it. Edwin allowed himself to take in the details of Lanthorne's bedroom.

It was half the size of his own in Grindling Close; the layout, though, was similar. The bed, the chest of drawers and even the chairs were more or less in the same place. He found this unnerving, but there was no desk, with its computer, radio and assorted gadgets. Instead of a wardrobe, Lanthorne had a pair of large cupboards set side by side in a deep recess. Edwin's arrival was so dramatic and confusing, he had no idea which of the cupboards he had come through.

All Lanthorne's furniture was roughly made and neither varnished nor painted, and the walls were so thinly splashed with whitewash, greywash really, that the stone showed through everywhere. There wasn't a single picture—in contrast to Edwin's bedroom, which looked like a poster gallery. The patch of rug only covered a fraction of the splintery floorboards. Edwin snagged his socks twice when he walked across them. The bed was hidden under blankets and Edwin imagined you had to burrow into them when you wanted to go to sleep.

It was as if his own bedroom, with its soft carpet and cheerful paintwork, had been transformed, by some spiteful magic, into a smelly garden shed.

The worst thing wasn't the smell, though; it was all so drab. The two cushions on the chairs and the blankets on the bed were either black or such dark shades of green or blue that they might as well have been black. Elsewhere it was grey, grey and even more grey, every-where—in the rug, the piece of clothing draped over the back of a chair, the corner of a pillow just visible at one end of the bed. It was this elimination of colour that made it so difficult for Edwin to meet Lanthorne's gaze. You needed proper cheeks and lips and eyes to look at when you were talking to someone, not features that seemed to have been drawn on a sheet of grey paper with a light pencil.

Edwin could see how much he himself stood out like a lightbulb, a genuine "Shiner".

His bare arms and legs were bright filaments in the gloom. His bare legs! Who ever heard of anyone starting an adventure in their underpants? But Edwin didn't want this adventure; he wanted an immediate return to the world he knew, where the worst thing that happened was Mandoline bursting into tears the moment he walked into a room.

"When can I go home?" he asked, in a sagging tone.

"I really don't know, Edwin. Soon, I expect. We'll need to look for a door."

"What about your cupboard door? I came through it, didn't I?"

"You came through the left-hand door, but I heard it snap shut afterwards. It won't let you back."

"I'll go through the right-hand door, then," said Edwin, brightening a little.

Lanthorne became very agitated.

"You can't open the right-hand cupboard, Edwin. Please. I'm keeping a special pet I rescued in there. My family don't know." He swallowed nervously. "I don't expect you have pets like it in your world. It's—"

"So what are we going to do?"

46

Lanthorne tried to smile encouragingly, but, to be encouraging, smiles need to be bright and surrounded by pink lips. Lanthorne's grey-lipped smile was neither of these, and Edwin wasn't reassured in the least.

Just at that moment, Edwin was convinced something wriggled against his behind, under the blanket. He jumped up. Lanthorne giggled.

"They won't hurt you."

They? "What are they?"

"They're very friendly. When I go to bed, they crawl about for a while and then they settle down."

"*What* are they?"

"Beetles, mostly. I tried giving them names, but there are so many of them."

Edwin leapt away from the bed. He liked having the cat curled up on his duvet at home, but he drew the line at beetles.

"I don't believe you heard the cupboard door snap shut," he said angrily. "I'm going to open it."

He rushed across the room to the left-hand cupboard and flung its door open. All that greeted him was assorted junk of an unidentifiable kind—not one of the cosy rooms in Grindling Close, which is what he'd been hoping. He slammed the door shut again.

Then he turned towards Lanthorne and glared. "You're lying about what's in the other cupboard. I think it's a door home, but you're just trying to keep me prisoner here because you haven't got any friends." He reached for the right-hand door handle, but Lanthorne was too quick for him.

"Edwin, don't! It's too dangerous." He jumped in front of his friend, snatched hold of his extended arm and forced it downwards. "It's a snarghe in there, Edwin. A snarghe. He's used to me, but you're different."

Edwin stormed across the room and threw himself heavily onto a chair. With the beetle-infested bed and the cupboard out of bounds, it was the only safe place left for him.

"Try to enjoy your visit. It's lovely to have you here, Edwin."

"I've got no shoes on and I'm only wearing my underpants. This isn't how we pay visits where I live."

"Wear some of *my* clothes. That'll be fun. My best clothes are in the cupboard with the snarghe, but the ones in my chest of drawers are almost as good."

"I don't think your clothes will be big enough for me," Edwin said weakly.

"I used to have an older brother," Lanthorne told him. "I haven't grown into his clothes yet. Try them."

Full of enthusiasm, Lanthorne busied himself pulling open drawers and rummaging through his shirts and pairs of trousers. He selected some and tried to hold them against Edwin, who refused to stand up and be measured. Agreeing to wear these dark, shapeless, hand-me-down clothes seemed like agreeing to take the place of Lanthorne's brother, as if he intended to stay there.

Suddenly Lanthorne dropped the shirt he was holding.

"More beetles?" asked Edwin.

Lanthorne put a finger to his lips.

There was a sound outside. Someone had come upstairs.

"You need to hide, Edwin. It might be my Auntie Necra. Perhaps she heard all the shouting and banging."

Edwin was about to argue that nobody's auntie was ever someone to be frightened of, but Lanthorne had already seized him tightly by the wrist and pulled him across to the right-hand cupboard.

"You'll have to hide in here." Lanthorne's voice was shaking.

"You mean the other cupboard."

"No, this one. The snarghe might protect you from Auntie Necra, if she finds you."

Edwin felt as if he had just been told that a crocodile was after him, so he needed to hide in a lion's cage.

"It won't like her. You don't know how terrifying she is. Once you're inside, stand absolutely still and keep facing the door." Lanthorne was gabbling his words extremely fast. "Don't upset it. And whatever you do, don't make the slightest noise."

In an instant, the cupboard door was opened. Edwin was somehow spun round and pushed in backwards by a hard little palm in his chest. He had never wanted to shout, "Arse and armpits!" so loudly in the whole of his life, but this wasn't the time or place.

When Lanthorne slammed the cupboard door shut, it almost hit Edwin in the face. He was in complete darkness and aware that it was a very deep cupboard with a lot of a space behind him. Somewhere in that space, something living made a rasping sound on the floor with its claws, and yawned. It sounded like the yawn from a very large mouth. Edwin inched forward and pressed his face against the door, but not hard enough to force it open. The creature behind him breathed out heavily, and Edwin felt puffs of air against the backs of his legs.

As the cupboard door slammed shut, so the bedroom door was thrown open. Two voices began a conversation in the room, but Edwin had difficulty making out what they were saying, because the cupboard door was such a snug fit. He thought he heard Lanthorne say, "Hello, Auntie," in a tone of false cheerfulness. The reply was sharp and more a collection of irritated sounds than actual words.

Edwin forced himself to concentrate on the conversation taking place in Lanthorne's bedroom. If he paid too much attention to what was happening behind him in the cupboard, he knew he would scream or faint. A large part of him was beginning to hope he would die of fright.

The mouth, which was breathing heavily, moved a lot nearer. *Concentrate*, he told himself. *Listen…*

Outside, Edwin could only pick out the odd word. The sharp voice said, "…you doing?" and Lanthorne said, "…tidying," and, "No, Auntie," several times.

Something rough and dripping was pressed against the back of Edwin's bare left leg. And then something equally rough and dripping made contact with the same spot on his bare right leg. They felt like tongues; scaly, mucousy tongues. What did this mean? Two heads? Two tongues in one head, or two snarghes? Edwin felt a scream building up in his throat. Very soon he wouldn't be able to control it.

Outside, someone whimpered in pain. Lanthorne. "No, I won't, Auntie." Then the whimpering again.

The tongues explored Edwin's legs slowly and carefully, peeling themselves away after each touch. They moved up to the hollows at the backs of his knees and then curled themselves around each knee, squeezing it tightly.

Edwin's scream was at the back of his throat now, and clamouring to be set free.

Outside, the auntie with the sharp voice was standing right next to the cupboard door. Edwin expected to be dragged out into the bedroom at any moment. And then what? Perhaps the snarghe would bite her head off. That might distract it from doing the same to him. The door handle shook.

"I've got a bad-tempered snarghe in there!" Lanthorne shouted. Edwin heard this clearly.

The auntie made a loud sound of disgust.

"Stupid child." She obviously did something else to Lanthorne because he squealed.

Footsteps clomped across the bedroom floor, then Edwin heard the door being banged shut. The snarghe jumped, and its tongues unwound from Edwin's knees.

The cupboard door flew open, and Edwin was hauled out.

Before he had time to look behind him, not that he wanted to, the cupboard door was firmly shut again. There were red marks on Edwin's legs, as if he had burnt or grazed himself. Lanthorne, for his part, had a set of dark-blue bruises by his left wrist. They were the unmistakable shape of fingers.

"You told her it was bad-tempered, and you let it lick me!" Edwin was furious.

"I was afraid it might do that."

"Was it being friendly?"

"It was identifying you."

"What for?"

"For later."

52

This wasn't information Edwin wanted to hear. "I've *got* to get home," he said.

Lanthorne led him back to the chair. "I'm glad nothing else happened to you in the cupboard. It would still have been better than facing my auntie."

"Don't," said Edwin.

"My Auntie Necra is completely horrible. She always wants to know what I'm doing. But she believed me when I said I was sorting out my clothes."

"Did she make those marks on your arm?"

"They'll fade."

What sort of family is this? Edwin asked himself. "Won't your mum be furious when she sees the bruises?"

"Auntie Necra sometimes pinches her too."

Edwin let the subject drop. "You *are* going to ask your friend to show me the way home?" he said.

"My friend Jugge helped me knock on those two doors into your world, but only after he'd done lots and lots of preparation. When it starts to get dark, we're going to visit him and ask him to do the same for you."

"It's pretty dark in here already."

In such half-light, Mrs Robbins would have switched on every lamp. Lanthorne didn't seem to notice how gloomy it was, and there was no sign of a light of any kind.

"This is only the afternoon, Edwin. We're not Shiners, like you. Dark here really is dark, especially now it's Dikembra."

53

"It's an afternoon in December back home too," said Edwin. He looked at his watch. *Three twenty-six, and they'll already be thinking about tea. Crumpets and jam by the fire.*

There was no point in dwelling on such thoughts, so Edwin returned to helping Lanthorne look for clothes big enough to fit him. This time, he agreed to stand up and be measured.

If going to see Lanthorne's special friend, the one with yet another peculiar name, was the only way to get home, he was prepared to do it, but he couldn't walk the streets half-naked.

Beetles in the bed, an auntie who tortured her nephew, and an unseen terror in the cupboard. Edwin wondered how long it would be before his mind simply gave way under it all.

5

Dikembra Plans

Although Lanthorne was happy to wear shorts in "Dikembra", Edwin was not. If it was this cold inside the house, then, outside, it must be like Alaska. He insisted on wearing the warmest pair of Lanthorne's brother's trousers they could find. The trouble was, every pair looked as if it had been made by someone unfashionable, on the day they sat on their glasses and broke them. Eventually, Edwin chose a pair which he tried to convince himself resembled a set of tracksuit bottoms fastened with a length of rough string. The colour was no colour at all and the cloth was heavy and chafed him. It was still better than walking around in his underwear.

Next, Lanthorne said, "Your shirt's too bright. No one here wears a white shirt with writing on."

In the circumstances, the slogan on Edwin's T shirt, *Stop staring, I know I'm SPECIAL*, was an unfunny joke. They decided to cover it with a short-sleeved grey shirt and a long top garment that Lanthorne called a coat. Edwin didn't really know what it was. It was knitted in thick, dark (possibly blue) wool and had an opening halfway down the front that was fastened with large wooden buttons. The sleeves were long and floppy, and it sported a hood. Edwin gave it a thorough shake before he agreed to put it on. It looked like prime beetle territory.

"You'll need to keep your head down when we go out," said Lanthorne. "Wear the hood like this." He pulled it down to the level of Edwin's nose. "And put these gloves on. Swarme must be sorry he left them behind."

"I don't suppose you have central heating in your house?" Edwin asked. Despite wearing the universe's most shapeless and outlandish suit of clothes, he was beginning to shiver.

Lanthorne looked puzzled. "Heating in the centre of what?" So the answer was no.

The biggest problem was shoes. Lanthorne had a spare pair which were several sizes too small. They looked like pixie shoes or the sort you might come up with after an unsuccessful afternoon in a handicraft class. They were not much more than leather bags tied tightly around the ankle.

"My father made them," explained Lanthorne. "He's not very good."

"Likewise."

"Like what?"

"I mean, like my dad. He's rubbish at making things. One of his favourite words is 'likewise'."

"My father's favourite word is 'pestofawoman'."

"Meaning your Auntie Necra?"

"Yes. She's always inviting herself to stay. Because Necra's her older sister, Mum feels she can't say no. Dad and me would say no every time."

"You should tell her to clear off and give her the bus fare home," Edwin suggested.

There were words here that Lanthorne didn't understand, but there wasn't time to ask questions. They had to concentrate on finding something Edwin could put on his feet.

"My mother bought my brother some expensive shoes for his Naming Day," Lanthorne said. "She still keeps them in her bedroom. I'll get them for you."

Edwin wondered what had happened to this older brother Lanthorne "used" to have. Did it mean he was dead? Perhaps something worse had happened to him. Better not to ask.

"I'm getting really hungry."

Even as he said it, Edwin imagined a dish of steaming—but still wriggling—beetles.

Stop it! They had to have bread and cheese, at least, or apples.

"You might not like our food, Edwin."

That was enough. "I'll wait till I get home, then."

Somehow, saying that made him feel more positive. Yes, he would return home, and, what's more, he would eat three complete meals in one go when he got there: roast chicken and chips, curry, burgers, trifle, apple crumble and custard, lemon meringue pie; the lot.

"In our house, you can smell when Mum's cooking lunch," he said.

"I've heard about cooking. My mother's never done it. It doesn't seem right to put burnt food into your mouth. We just let our food ripen."

Edwin was confused. You let tomatoes and bananas ripen, so why did Lanthorne warn him? Did they just live on fruit or salads, like some of his mum's friends? And if so, what was the problem? *If I don't get home today, I'm sure I'll starve,* he thought. His fragment of optimism faded.

"I'm going to leave you for a while," said Lanthorne.

Edwin panicked. "I don't want to be here on my own." There was a snarghe in the cupboard, a tribe of beetles in the bed and a pinching aunt on the prowl. He couldn't possibly be safe.

"You need the shoes and I'm going to smear your face with dirt. Even with the hood pulled down, you're

58

shining too much. There's some good mud by the privye. You can get into my bed, if you like, while I'm gone."

There was no chance of that. And Edwin was about to have his face daubed with... *No, don't think about it.*

"And remember—"

"I know. Don't make the slightest noise."

"My mother and Auntie Necra like to sit in the living room, chatting, in the afternoon. Well, Auntie Necra does most of the talking. Dad's at the stoneyarde, so I shouldn't have a problem getting the shoes unless Mum's hidden them. If it all goes wrong, I'll shout out your name and you must run away as far as you can go."

Edwin felt crushed. Where could he run safely in this alien world, in his socks? It would be simpler to go into the cupboard, give the snarghe a hefty kick and let the creature end it all.

Lanthorne left the bedroom, and Edwin sat down on the chair, feeling colder by the minute. He hadn't dared look out of the small window and didn't do so now. The glass was a swirly yellow that reminded him of wee, which was somehow predictable. Not much light came in, and it was growing less, a winter afternoon drawing towards its end.

When the shivers began to rattle his teeth, and snuggling into the hoodie did no good at all, Edwin looked across the room at Lanthorne's bed. Burrow into it he certainly wouldn't, but he might be able to relieve it

59

of one of its blankets. On tiptoe, he went over to the bed and slapped one corner of the blankets very hard. He hoped any nearby beetles would think they were under attack and scurry away to the farthest corner of the bed. It was a dull sort of slap, not a sharp one, because the thickness of the covers absorbed the sound. All the same, he stood absolutely still, his ears pricked. There was no hint of dreadful Auntie Necra's footsteps on the stairs, but, in its cupboard, the snarghe sneezed twice. The sneezes were squeaky rather than loud, but they blew out so much air the cupboard door rattled. Edwin was afraid it would fly open.

These might be the last moments of my life, he thought. Fearing that razor-like teeth and claws were about to sink deeply into him, he turned slowly round. The cupboard was still shut. He was safe. After peeling the top blanket off the bed, he gave it a thorough shake and carried it back to his chair, where he wrapped it around him. It reduced the shivers to an acceptable level.

But Edwin's worries weren't so easily dealt with. He couldn't stop thinking about the snarghe, so few feet away. Had he heard two heads sneezing one after the other, or one head with an uncomfortable amount of dust in its single nose? Either way, the snarghe was a creature Edwin intended never to meet again.

By the time Lanthorne returned, only twenty minutes later, Edwin was thoroughly sick of his dismal thoughts. He tried to be enthusiastic about the giant pair of sandals Lanthorne claimed he'd retrieved at great risk. They slid about on Edwin's feet when he experimented with walking in them. A drawstring fastened them rather than buckles, and no amount of tugging on it could make the sandals seem any narrower. He knew he would never be able to run in them if danger threatened, and how far could he get trying to sprint in his socks?

"Your brother had enormous feet."

"He was fifteen when..."

"And I'm not smearing that on my face. It stinks."

Lanthorne was holding out a small wooden cup containing a dark and sticky substance.

"Edwin, this is the best dirt. We grow things in it."

"It's a cup of poo. Why don't you admit it?"

"It's from the garden, not from someone's bottom. I promise."

"I'm still not putting it on my face till we get outside. *Our* garden doesn't smell like that and my dad says his tomatoes are still fantastic."

"There won't be time when we get outside. Now please stand still."

Edwin submitted to having his face plastered thickly with what Lanthorne kept promising was ordinary garden dirt. When a line of gunge is spread under your nose like the world's vilest moustache, Edwin

61

discovered that you can't close your nostrils against the smell. He had to keep telling himself, *It's for my own good*. Complaining wasn't any help because he ran the risk of letting it into his mouth. He remembered a bird-poo-in-the-hair bullying incident at school last year and now knew exactly what the victim felt. He regretted having laughed.

"I've brought you something else," said Lanthorne. "Something very special to me. Think of my name and then guess what I'm hiding behind my back."

Edwin was not in the mood for a guessing game. Condemned men about to face execution don't play I spy and, right now, he wasn't going to play a childish game either. "I give up," he said immediately.

Lanthorne looked crestfallen. "Have just one guess."

"Chicken curry with poppadoms."

These words were a completely foreign language to Lanthorne. "Look," he said proudly, holding up a tiny lantern, a square, old-fashioned one with shutters made of a brownish material. "This is how I got my name."

"From a lantern?"

"No, a *lanthorne*." He opened one of the shutters, revealing a stub of candle. "The sides are made of slices of a cow's *horn*. But *you'll* have to light it when the time comes. I'm still a little frightened of flames."

"Why do you have the same name as a lantern? I mean, *lanthorne*?"

"It's like this..." Happy to be able to tell his guest a story, Lanthorne made himself comfortable on the floor in front of Edwin, who sat on a chair. "*Your* parents chose *your* name, didn't they?"

"Of course," said Edwin.

"And where did they get that name from?"

"It's a Robbins family name. My grandfather and his father were both called Edwin. Lots of people name babies after someone famous on the telly, or footballers."

Lanthorne looked puzzled. More strange words. "Here, a father gives his new baby the name of the first thing he sees after the baby is born."

"I'm surprised every baby isn't called *Lady'sfrontbottom*, then," said Edwin.

They both rocked with laughter but made as little noise as they could, because it might bring Auntie Necra snooping again.

"Your father wasn't *in the room* when you were born, was he?" Lanthorne asked in disbelief.

"*And* when my sister Mandoline was born. He said he felt faint for a week afterwards."

"Our fathers wait outside. Then, when they're told the baby has been born, they choose its name from the last thing they were looking at. I was born at night and my father was carrying a lanthorne."

"If he was outside, he could have been looking at a worm or some dog mess on the pavement."

63

"Like the father of poor Uncle Tarde."

Edwin thought about this name for a moment. "Oh, I get it," he said. "Uncle *Turd*. He must have hated his dad."

They started laughing again.

"I'd choose the name beforehand and then pretend I'd seen it."

"You mustn't lie about it," said Lanthorne firmly. "The trick is to make sure you only look at nice things. My friend's name is Jugge because his father had just gone into the kitchen, and they called my brother Swarme."

"As in, a swarm of bees?"

"No, a swarme of blow flies. He was born in the month of Angist."

Edwin inspected his watch again. It was rude to cut across Lanthorne's story, but he was feeling desperate. "Is it time to leave yet?" he asked.

"I think so," said Lanthorne. "It must be dark enough by now, but not too dark. I had to tell my mum I want to visit my friend Jugge. She was in the middle of an argument with Auntie Necra, so it's a good thing we're leaving the house. They both ask me to side with them when they quarrel, and I get pulled about a lot."

"Don't your parents stand up for you?"

Lanthorne didn't answer. He took a step towards the door and slipped on a hooded top similar to the one so unwillingly sported by Edwin, who took this as a sign for him to follow.

"Wait!" said Lanthorne, turning and catching his arm. "We'll need this." He handed Edwin the lanthorne and a large, crude match, together with a stone which he took out of his pocket.

Edwin set the lanthorne down on top of the chest of drawers and opened the shutter. As he struck the blob of a match head against the piece of stone, he knew he needed to light the miserable little piece of candle very carefully if he wanted to be sure they had some light at least. Lanthorne had turned his back while this was going on, but he still flinched when the match flared into life.

"If you hate flames so much, how could you bear to send me those letters up a chimney?" Edwin asked him.

"It's only the smoke you need, not the flames," said Lanthorne. "Jugge posted the letters for me anyway. Come on. Let's get going. I'll have a look out on the stairs first. You can never tell with my auntie. She heard me asking my mother if I could go out at this time of day. If it's safe, you wait outside the door while I let the snarghe out. If it has to stay in the cupboard much longer, it'll begin to howl."

There was no sign of Lanthorne's mother or Auntie Necra, who were presumably still at loggerheads, so Edwin was able to tiptoe out onto the landing, which had no windows and was completely dark. The lanthorne didn't so much light up the landing and the top stairs as create a series of unsettling shadows. Edwin felt he might have been better off without it. He could tell that Lanthorne had opened the door of the cupboard in his bedroom, because there was a sound of clawed feet scampering across the floor. This was followed by alternate sniffing and grunting sounds—made by separate mouths taking it in turns, perhaps.

Lanthorne could be heard scolding the animal and then Edwin recognized the teeth-on-edge screech of claws being dragged reluctantly away from the door. He moved as far across the landing as he could, hoping to take every trace of his scent with him. He was still very concerned about what Lanthorne meant when he said the snarghe was "identifying" him "for later". That later hadn't better be now.

"If you know what to say to a snarghe, it'll do anything you want," said Lanthorne, when he finally appeared. "But it can't abide sarcasm. Auntie Necra is in for a horrible shock if she sneaks into my room uninvited. This one has a taste for fingers and toes." He sniggered.

The two boys made their way carefully down the staircase, Edwin following closely behind his friend, who carried the lanthorne. Its faint circle of light hardly managed to include the pair of them.

6

Jugge

There were no street lamps or any spillage of light from windows, and their lanthorne might as well not have been lit. Such light as there was came from the sky, a narrow strip of grey streaked with bruised yellow that was turning darker as Edwin looked up at it. In the unbroken gloom, he couldn't see very far in any direction. The boys appeared to be in a narrow lane rather than a street, and all the houses opened straight onto it. They didn't even look like separate houses, but seemed to be part of a continuous greystone block, two storeys high, with the occasional narrow door and a few windows like portholes. There was a strong sense of people shutting themselves away and keeping very still and quiet if a stranger knocked.

"Don't let me get lost," Edwin said plaintively.

"It's not far."

They walked to the end of the lane without meeting anyone and then turned right and left along two more narrow and shadowy passages. Underfoot, it felt like a hard earth track rather than a proper road surface and there were no pavements. If Landarn was London in another form, Edwin felt they hadn't made a very good job of it.

"Keep your head right down," said Lanthorne. "You don't realize how much you're shining."

"No, I don't. My face is plastered with muck!"

"We're going to pass through the big streets soon, so be extra careful."

The "big streets" turned out to be hardly any wider or more impressive. There were pavements of sorts and a few people walking on them. It was practically dark and they all wore hooded clothing, so Edwin had no idea what they looked like. Occasionally, they greeted Lanthorne, two words spoken in passing and without a slowing down of their pace.

"Well met."

Each time, Lanthorne replied softly, "Be safe onwards," a worrying response if ever there was one, suggesting that something terrible was likely to befall you quite soon.

So near Christmas, at home, the streets would be thronged and the shops ablaze. As the two boys scurried along, Edwin glimpsed what might have passed for shops—buildings with largish windows resolutely shuttered against the night. The near silence was uncomfortable, and he was very conscious of the *slap-slap* he made with each step in the badly fitting sandals.

As they turned one street corner, an almighty gust of wind blew straight into their faces. It was so strong it forced Edwin's hood back, revealing a lot of his face. Lanthorne gasped, reached up and yanked the hood down so far that Edwin now had no idea at all of where he was going. Effectively blind, he stumbled and stubbed his toes, so he was in a rebellious and angry mood when they eventually came to a halt.

Edwin lifted his head and saw a low, narrow door, identical to the one which opened into Lanthorne's house. It had the same unvarnished planks of wood, with no knocker or letter box. Was this an unpleasant trick? Had he trailed around in the dark, tripping over his feet every second step, just to arrive back where they started?

Lanthorne moved up to the door and knocked in a pattern that Edwin could barely hear.

"You never know who's listening," Lanthorne said. "It's our secret knock."

"I couldn't hear it and I'm only two feet away."

Lanthorne put his finger to his lips. "You mustn't shout about secrets."

"I'm not shouting!" Edwin shouted.

Lanthorne repeated the timid pattern of knocks. In a more encouraging, but still quiet, voice he said, "Don't worry about the Whisperers. It's their time."

Edwin had just begun to notice how the falling of complete darkness brought unsettling noises with it. They were different from that of a breeze springing up and using the lane as a shortcut. These were sounds that moved up and down the fronts of the houses, attaching themselves to the stones and feeling for windows that weren't properly closed. Snatches of breath puffed out of lips Edwin could sense but not see. They were beginning to circle around the boys as Lanthorne knocked for a third time. Clammy fingers of air pressed a hollow in Edwin's cheek. Something invisible hissed and pushed his nose to one side.

"Get off!" he yelled and, throwing himself at the door, banged on it with his fist as powerfully as he could. "Jugge, let us in!"

The sharp explosion of sound blew the whispering airs away. Lanthorne stood speechless, and still the door didn't open. But the whispering was quickly closing around them again, and it was even closer. Edwin felt that there were now words in the hiss and rustle. Were they questions, or approving comments like, "This one looks tasty"?

He tried to swat them away like summer gnats. All Lanthorne did, meanwhile, was to press his ear against the door. Edwin was too busy swatting and *get off*-ing to hear a pattern of tapping from inside and Lanthorne's reply.

Suddenly a rectangle of the dimmest light appeared where the door had been. There was determined pressure on Edwin's arm and a moment later the boys were inside.

"Lanthorne, why so late?" asked Jugge. "Is it your Auntie Necra again?"

"This is Edwin, my Shiner friend," Lanthorne said excitedly. "He suddenly came through a door into my bedroom. Edwin, this is my friend Jugge. He's the cleverest person in Landarn."

There was silence as Jugge stared at Edwin open-mouthed. He gasped when Lanthorne pulled back Edwin's hood and revealed his face. Despite the mud daubed all over it, his Shinerness glowed through.

"Such an honour. Edwin. Thank you. Thank you," said Jugge.

He took their lanthorne, blew it out and led the boys down a short corridor as rough and bare as the inside of Lanthorne's home. At the end was a fairly large room that was bright in comparison with what Edwin had seen of Lanthorne's house, but, compared with Mrs Robbins's collection of lamps, it was seriously underlit and too full of dark corners.

Lanthorne leant over to Edwin and whispered, "You'll like Jugge's house. He's very modern. That's why it's so much brighter."

71

You could have fooled me, Edwin thought. *It's almost as shadowy and strange as everywhere else. And I don't like the look of Jugge. I wish he'd stop staring at me and licking his lips.*

Edwin hadn't given much thought as to how old Jugge was likely to be, but he was still surprised to see that Lanthorne's special friend was apparently no older than his own cousin Alastair, who was twenty-eight. Or perhaps people aged differently in this world, and Jugge was really 278 and Lanthorne a mere thirty-two. Jugge stood a handful of inches taller than Edwin and was so thin that there was hardly room for the various features on his face. His skin had the same underlying greyness as Lanthorne's, as if they had both stepped out of a poorly printed black and white photograph, but, when he bowed his head slightly to give Edwin a proper welcome, touches of red were visible at the tops of his cheeks.

"Allow me to shake the hand of a creature of legend, a Shiner boy."

Jugge stepped towards Edwin, who had no choice but to allow Jugge to wrap his fingers around his own. They were twitchy, fidgety fingers, like the tentacles of a sea anemone, but their grip was tight and Edwin pulled his hand away as soon as he could.

"People here have stopped believing in Shiners," said Jugge. "But I knew. I always knew. And here you are, standing in front of me, even brighter than all the tales said."

Jugge was wearing loose trousers of an indeterminate dark colour and a grey shirt that was similarly baggy, as if to disguise how scraggy or skeletal his body was. Two details about him stood out. Edwin had been trying not to stare at them from the moment Jugge stood in enough light for them to be seen clearly.

Over his shirt, he had on a sort of tank top, knitted from bright blue and yellow wool. It was a horrible garment, an atrocity in fact. The point was that it was colourful—made in garish, loud colours—and Edwin wondered what Jugge was trying to say by wearing it. Did he only wear it secretly at home? In the street, everybody was bound to stare. Such colours might even be illegal. And it had come from his own world, Edwin was certain.

Jugge's hairstyle was also a peculiar statement. Around his ears it was as grey as Lanthorne's dull little mop, but he had slicked it down over the top of his head so that he could make a kind of parting. Whatever he had used, some kind of grease, it made his hair look darker and sleeker.

He's pretending he's one of us, thought Edwin. He wasn't sure whether to smile or shiver at this.

Three candle stubs set in recesses at head height each gave out a little more light than their lanthorne had, and in the small grate a fire smouldered. It was a feeble excuse for a fire, with only two visible flames.

Jugge stood in the middle of the room and flicked out his arms in a *Ta-da!* kind of movement, as if to say, "I know, I know. I couldn't make it more Shinery if I tried." He looked down at the pattern on his tank top and Edwin took the hint.

"Super jumper," said Edwin. "My dad's got one in the very same colours."

Jugge obviously appreciated the compliment. "I've always wondered about the design," he said. "Is it a fat and jolly man with a peculiar face?"

"It's Winnie the Pooh."

"A hero?"

"Sort of."

"It's supposed to have come from your world, years ago. I had to pay a lot of money for it, even though nobody believed it was genuine. So, is it?"

"Looks like it," said Edwin.

"Jugge tracks down Shiner objects," said Lanthorne proudly.

"Wow," said Edwin.

"Yes, his collection is the best in Landarn."

For a moment, Jugge looked very intensely at Edwin. The pupils of his eyes were dark in comparison to Lanthorne's and, unlike Lanthorne's, they actually gleamed. It was a steady, sharp gleam and definitely not a friendly twinkle. Edwin turned away and looked at the fire. He longed to stir it up with a poker and bring some life to the room, which was as cosy as a rarely used cupboard.

"Let's sit down and have a wonderful chat," said Jugge. "There are so many questions I told myself I would ask a Shiner, if I was ever lucky enough to meet one."

He motioned for Edwin to sit in the chair nearest the fire. It was crudely made and had a single, uncomfortable cushion.

"You don't mind me calling you a Shiner, do you? It isn't meant to be..."

"Racist," said Edwin, anxious to finish the sentence and get on to talk of going home. "No, I don't mind. What do I call *you*?"

Jugge looked across the room to Lanthorne, who had curled up on a hard chair some way from the fire. "What are we, Lanthorne? What have you told your excellent new friend about us?"

Lanthorne gazed down at the patch of floor beneath his feet and shifted his position on his chair. Edwin wasn't at all happy with the silence that followed. He felt he was being excluded from really important information, a kind of password that it was vital for him to know.

"I told him my Auntie Necra's completely horrible and we can't control her," said Lanthorne suddenly, breaking the silence. "I told him we're just us." He seemed relieved to have come up with this particular answer.

Jugge took a stool and placed it in front of Edwin. He sat down on it, much too close for Edwin's liking.

"I enjoy sitting by the fire, looking into the flames," he said as if it were something special. "I enjoy candle flames too."

"Not like me," called Lanthorne. "I need a lot more practice with bare flames."

"From time to time you hear about sightings of Shiners," said Jugge, "but young Master Edwin here is the best evidence for them, for I don't know how many years. And he's walked right into my living room as if it was nothing special. I expect that over on your side you have legends and stories about fantastic creatures too."

He's fishing for something, Edwin thought. *But I don't know what.* He pondered for a moment and then said, "People go looking for yetis."

"Yettyes!" Jugge and Lanthorne cried out at the same time.

"They're real enough," said Jugge. "A nest of them must have crossed over into your world and got stuck there. Nasty, bitey things. Best avoided."

"If anyone finds one, they'll get a nasty shock, then," Edwin said. He edged further back in his chair and as far away from Jugge as he could manage without making it too pointed. Jugge had the same staleness about

76

him as Lanthorne—more, in fact, because he was an adult—and his excitement at meeting a Shiner caused him to breathe in and out very deeply. Edwin couldn't help flinching at each sour out-breath. He knew that if he didn't speak forcefully now he could find himself trapped into talking for hours.

"Lanthorne promised you would help me get home," he said in a voice he knew sounded impatient and bratty. He didn't care. His mother might say, "Never judge until you are really sure," but she hadn't smelt anyone like Jugge or been gleamed at by those dark eyes. The sooner he got out of there the better.

"Of course, of course," said Jugge, "but you won't mind if I try to get right to the heart of a Shiner first."

Edwin was now pressed as hard against the back of the chair as he could be. He didn't like this talk of hearts. What an odd thing to say. Had Lanthorne betrayed him, and was this the end of the road?

"I expect you're wondering how these doors between our two worlds work," Jugge said.

Edwin wasn't wondering about it at all at that particular moment, but he thought it would be sensible to play along for a while.

"They're amazing," he said.

"It's a complicated story."

"My dad—" Edwin began, but Jugge cut his sentence short.

"For hundreds and hundreds of years," he continued, "there were lots of doors, but then the people in your world found ways of closing them."

"Why?" Edwin couldn't help asking.

"Yes, why?" interrupted Lanthorne. Then he quickly said, "Oh," as if he had remembered a very good reason.

Jugge clenched his long fingers in annoyance. He went on with what he was saying without bothering to answer Edwin's question. "Your people discovered special words of closure, and whenever a door opened they spoke them. They thought they had closed all the doors for ever, but these special words are wearing thin." He stared into Edwin's face with greater intensity. "Have you ever noticed doors suddenly flying open for no apparent reason?"

"Yes, but it's the wind," Edwin replied. He wasn't enjoying this conversation.

Jugge sniggered. "No, it's the special words getting thinner and thinner. At the moment, they're mostly only thin enough to allow doors to open but not to let people through."

"Then how did..."

Jugge folded his arms smugly. "I found some other words and I gave the doors that extra push they needed. It wasn't easy. I'll admit that."

"He was exhausted afterwards," Lanthorne added, as if Jugge had done something impressive or brave.

"The doors are capricious," Jugge said slowly, like someone sharing a great secret.

"They can be very choosy. It's my considered conclusion that they're annoyed at being closed for so long and so they're getting their revenge by playing tricks." He smiled at the idea of the sheer spitefulness of the doors. The smile was followed by a long sigh of admiration.

Edwin instinctively turned away from yet more sour breath, but he saw a chance to interrupt Jugge's tale with what he had tried to say before.

"My dad's a hero," he blurted out, "just like Winnie the Pooh on your top. He gets very angry if I stay out too late. He doesn't know I'm here." That wasn't a good thing to admit. "If you know all these other words, can you use them and find me a door NOW, please?" He tried to sound as polite and needy as he could. "My parents will be very worried."

"I'm sure they will."

"You're not very helpful!" Edwin didn't care that he'd shouted; his anxiety had reached that stage. "Why won't you help me go through a door?" *And never, NEVER come back.*

"I was really looking forward to this chat," said Jugge. There was a new edge to his voice. "You could almost say I've been looking forward to it all my life. And all you want to do is go home." He stood up.

Edwin stood up too.

Jugge gestured around him. "You ought to feel at home here. There's a fire and plenty of light and two rugs on the floor. Not like the old days." He threw a fierce look at Lanthorne, who jumped off his chair with a little squeal and hurried to stand beside his friend.

It's taken you long enough, thought Edwin.

Jugge kicked over his stool and went and stood by the far wall, his arms crossed and his expression a resentful glower. Edwin glowered back. He couldn't help noticing that Jugge's slicked-down hair was beginning to spring back up, hair by hair, until a whole tuft was free. Was he seeing the real Jugge emerge from behind a Winnie the Pooh mask?

"Try to be more friendly," Lanthorne said quietly. "Jugge's the only one who can help you."

Edwin was beyond being friendly. "He found *you* a door. Why can't he use those same words and find me a door too?"

Lanthorne prodded him.

"My dad's twice your size," Edwin snapped. "You wouldn't last five minutes."

Lanthorne prodded him harder.

"We were very lucky finding doors for Lanthorne," said Jugge. "First of all, I had to search for old books. They're difficult to locate and their owners are usually afraid to let you have them. You see, most people in our world are glad we don't have contact with Shiners any more. They believe you're monsters who enjoy burning people to ash and then walk away laughing."

"That's not what Jugge and I think," Lanthorne chimed in. "We know the truth about you. You're ordinary people like us, who happen to be a bit different."

Jugge clearly hated being interrupted when he was showing off about his research. He gave Lanthorne a look which made this clear.

"When you have tracked the books down," Jugge continued, "what they say is never clear. There are hints and all sorts of false clues, but I was able to read between the lines."

"Yes, Jug—" Lanthorne was silenced with another look.

"Lanthorne was my great experiment. I made a list of all the special words I could find and said them in enough different ways, until I managed to push him through that first door."

How brave, Edwin thought to himself. *Trying it out on a kid first.*

"We tried door after door before I ended up in your garden," said Lanthorne. "It has to be the right door with the right words. That's ever so hard. The first time we nearly managed it, you were afraid and didn't like to open the door. I was afraid too. I wondered if you'd turn me to cinders. The second time, I only opened the door a little, because it was so bright outside. I closed it again, but somehow I'd managed to come through anyway. Didn't we have a good time in your garden house?"

"It wasn't a house. It was a mucky shed," Edwin said gruffly.

"The doors appear *because* you want them," said Jugge, who looked irritated at being ignored. "But not always *when* and *where* you want them. I think I might be building up a kind of relationship with them. I'm getting a *feel*, you could say. If I can earn their trust, perhaps they'll let me open them whenever I want. That would make me really special."

"For some reason I don't understand, they seem to be interested in you."

Edwin didn't like the sound of this. He made a harrumphing sound and renewed his glower.

"Why don't I get us something to eat?" said Lanthorne.

Jugge laughed mockingly. "Shall we prepare your new friend a feast, Lanthorne? I think he'll find our food very interesting."

I'm not going to be sidetracked into a discussion about food. "I'm not hungry," said Edwin.

Jugge laughed more loudly.

Once someone starts cackling, thought Edwin, *it's time to move.* He'd had all he could take of this world where he was surrounded by the constant smell of things his own world flushed away.

82

"Jugge could show you some of his precious books about Shiners," Lanthorne began, but Edwin was off.

He rushed to the door leading into the corridor. "Jugge says let me go home!" he shouted at whatever power it was that seemed to be in control of the doors. Hoping that they had heard, he wrenched the door open.

On the other side, there was the same gloomy corridor as earlier. Edwin turned to face Lanthorne and Jugge. The expression on their faces showed that they were wondering what he was going to do next. Edwin was wondering this too. All he could think of was to pull off his coat and whirl it round his head, which he did. Lanthorne and Jugge flinched, but didn't otherwise move. Edwin threw the coat in Jugge's direction and rushed towards a second door.

"Jugge says let me please go home!" The door-controllers still weren't listening. Edwin was faced with a second, darker corridor. Down this to yet another door. He was now in the kitchen, or what passed for the kitchen.

A single, faint candle hardly revealed a table, two chairs and a shelf with a few jars and plates. Edwin was convinced that if he stood still for a moment, he would break down. He needed to keep rushing about and pulling open doors. How could the door home not appear, when every molecule inside him was screaming for it to happen?

Two doors led off the kitchen. These were his last hope. The first let out into a yard at the back of the house. Edwin pulled back from a wall of utter darkness and left the door swinging on its hinges. That left only the narrow door made of two long planks. On the verge of tears, Edwin wrenched it open and was knocked backwards by the most aggressive and putrid smell he could ever imagine. It was as if the essence of every rotten thing in the world had been bottled and stored in that cupboard, ready for him to open the door and let it out. He was smacked in the face so hard by the smell that it took him a moment or two to recover his balance and slam the door shut. The stink went right up into his head, like fingers being pushed up his nose and into his brain. Who on earth could bear to have such nastiness in their house?

Once the smell was released, it congealed in the air to a kind of sheet that draped itself over every part of Edwin. He felt himself drowning in the sheer disgustingness of it. His arms flapped without co-ordination, as if he were trying to swim up to a surface he couldn't reach. Each gasp took more of the smell into his lungs, but as he was on the verge of fainting, he was hauled out of the kitchen and back into Jugge's living room, where he collapsed to his knees.

"A good thing I followed you," said Lanthorne.

Edwin looked up at his friend. He didn't have enough control of his breathing to speak.

"Fetch him a drink of water," said Jugge.

Edwin shook his head violently. He didn't want anything from that kitchen, because it would be tainted by the stink to end all stinks. He slumped down further and lay for some time with his face buried in his arms. The touch and smell of his own skin was reassuring. Lanthorne prodded him occasionally, and eventually Edwin sat up and found he had part of his voice back.

"What was in that cupboard? It all looked rotten. You know, liquid rotten. The most disgusting-looking things you could ever imagine."

"Jugge's even better at ripening food than my mum," Lanthorne said cheerfully.

"That wasn't ripe," said Edwin in disbelief. "It had all gone totally bad."

Even these few sentences brought back a vivid picture of the interior of Jugge's pantry: dishes that were oozing, wriggling, mouldering; plates on which slabs of food were turning to putrescent mush or green and black gardens of fur. Every item was months beyond its burying date. You could have poisoned an entire town with them.

"If you're sure you don't like our food," said Lanthorne helpfully, "you could bring some of your squashed-fly biscuits with you, next time you come."

Next time? Lanthorne had to be joking.

"I couldn't find a door. Why not?" Edwin asked, as he was led back to his chair.

"I don't know," replied Jugge. "I wouldn't be surprised if the doors were just enjoying playing about with you."

Edwin closed his eyes. He was beginning to think he must have died and not noticed it. Perhaps he had fallen down the stairs at home and broken his neck. This was his punishment for not welcoming Mandoline into the family. Hell was eternal, wasn't it? Such a long punishment for such a little crime. If he were forced to stay here, would there come a time when he had no option but to scoop up the putrid liquids in the pantry and tell himself they were delicious?

"You've got to help me find some more doors, Lanthorne." A note of serious anger entered Edwin's voice. "You said your wise friend Jugge would get me home. He's been useless."

"I'm giving my full attention to the problem, Edwin," said Jugge. "So stop being so rude to me."

"Sorry."

"If you really are a natural door-opener, there are more doors upstairs. Let's try those. If we all concentrate hard, we might be lucky. You mustn't look as if you're trying to bully them, though. Doors expect politeness."

Edwin stood up. "Let's start now."

Suddenly there was a tremendous crash against Jugge's front door, making all three of them jump. The crash was followed by violent knocking punctuated by loud, angry scratches.

"Lanthorne, I know you're in there. And I know what you're up to. Open this door. Now!"

"Auntie Necra," whimpered Lanthorne.

Jugge tried to control the trembling in his voice. "I'll speak to her through the door," he said. "I'll tell her you went to visit another friend half an hour ago."

"Lanthorne! I know who you've got in there. I've read your letters." There was more scratching than knocking now.

Lanthorne emitted a continuous low moaning, and Jugge's fingers wrapped themselves around each other. Neither he nor Lanthorne moved a single step.

If they couldn't deal with the situation, then Edwin would. He set off towards the front door too suddenly for them to stop him. By the time he grasped the door handle, the word "No!" was only just beginning to form on their horrified lips.

Edwin flung the door open and jumped out. He was mostly expecting to collide with Lanthorne's terrifying Auntie Necra. If he could manage it, he hoped to brush her aside and run down the street, opening every door he could find.

Instead of encountering a furious woman, he found himself standing in a landscape over which night had fallen.

7

The Worst Thing Imaginable

Edwin suspected that he was home, or, at least, back in his own world.

It was dark and cold, but there were stars—sharp, bright points of light that told him he could stand still and collect himself, because things were all right now. His eyes wandered across the sky, half recognizing the larger constellations. He took a deep breath, and then another. The air smelt clean, with undertones of leaves and frost. His own world, it didn't matter where.

Well, perhaps it did. He was wearing Swarme's sandals, and his toes soon felt pinched by the cold. He had left the coat in Jugge's house, and the shirt Lanthorne gave him wasn't exactly fleece-lined. Edwin hoped he hadn't come through the door into Scotland, say, or anywhere miles from his house.

He was in a wide area, surrounded by dark, irregular shapes—shapes that showed no sign of movement, so it was unlikely they were alive and waiting to pounce on him. Unlikely, but not impossible.

Edwin moved backwards a couple of steps, until he bumped into the edge of the small building whose door had provided his passage home. He jumped away again. There was no point in escaping from Lanthorne's rotten world only to fall back into it by mistake. It didn't require any effort to recall the dangerous eyes and frightening mouth of the woman he had swept past as he escaped. Auntie Necra. Her long-fingered hands had reached out to snatch at him. The door behind him belonged to a small building no bigger than the shed in his own garden. To think that something so insignificant could take you so far...

In the distance, streetlights shone yellow and huge, further proof he was in a world where the people didn't shrink away from brightness. From time to time, Edwin heard the unmistakable sound of a car engine. If he moved a few paces in any direction and flapped his arms, he encountered plants, some with leaves as broad as those on a cabbage. There were worse places to pop up in than a vegetable garden. Suddenly, a violent, thundering sound, close at hand and yet up in the air, made him jump and cry out. He fell to his knees and put his hands over his ears. For a second or two he thought a monstrous, glowing caterpillar had launched itself through the air towards him. Then he fell sideways onto the ground, chuckling with relief. It was nothing more than a commuter train rattling along the top of its embankment, taking people home from work or Christmas shopping.

As the train raced by, its light had swept over the landscape below the track. Edwin chuckled again, because he'd caught a glimpse of other sheds dotted here and there and rows of winter greens. He had crossed over into the allotment only a few streets from his house.

Once the train had gone, the details around Edwin merged into the darkness again. He couldn't see a direct path to the roadway, with its oh-so-welcome street-lights, but, if he looked about him until he found the beginning of any path, he could walk carefully along it, taking every turning that led in the direction he wanted.

Ten minutes later, Mrs Robbins was asking, "Edwin, what on earth are you doing outside so late? It's nearly seven."

He had been trying to creep back into the house unnoticed and didn't immediately have an answer for his mother.

"Your radio's been playing all afternoon. Were you trying to trick me?" Mrs Robbins's voice was not a pleased one.

"I called out to you when I went out. You were probably talking to Mandoline and didn't notice."

This was a familiar tactic of Edwin's: when you're in the wrong, try to make your accuser feel guilty.

"You should have made sure I heard you. It's pitch dark out there. You know how much I worry." His mother threw the guilt straight back at him. Edwin didn't feel he could walk away, with her on the verge of being seriously angry.

"Sorry, Mum. I did call out to you. Honest. I must have forgotten to switch off the radio."

As he stood hesitantly by the back door, Edwin couldn't help being very aware of how odd he looked. The kitchen spotlights glared at him and picked out all the peculiarities in his borrowed clothes. In a room sweet with the smell of freshly tumbled laundry and the spicy casserole in the oven, he was acutely aware of stinking like nothing on earth—literally. Edwin knew just how much the smell of the contents of Jugge's pantry had stuck to him. There was no way his mother wouldn't notice and pass comment.

"Where did you get those awful clothes?"

"I borrowed them from my friend."

"What's wrong with your own clothes? These smell as if he found them at the bottom of a very old dustbin."

"I didn't want to ruin what I was wearing. We've been crawling about under the hedges round the playing field."

"Why, in heaven's name?"

"My friend..."

"Who is this friend?"

"Code name L. I'm E. He's got a book about the SAS. We were copying their techniques. You can't let the enemy spot you."

"SAS? That's a bit outside your comfort zone, isn't it?"

"I have previously undiscovered talents."

Edwin's mouth seemed to be working on automatic pilot. He was surprised how quickly his answers came out.

"Can't you smell yourself?" his mother asked.

"SAS operatives don't care about personal comfort."

"Or personal hygiene, apparently. Where were you being an operative? Down a sewer?"

"Sorry, that's classified information."

"For heaven's sake, get those clothes off. They're infecting my kitchen. You can tell your friend code-named L to collect them first thing tomorrow. He can bring your clothes back at the same time. I notice you don't have them with you. How can you bear to wear such an appalling outfit?"

"I'd do anything for my country."

"Stop trying to be smart, Edwin. I've a good mind to ask Dad to scrub you."

"Mum, I'm twelve years old. I don't do *bath time* any more. I can scrub myself."

Edwin was made to drape himself in a couple of old towels and undress by the back door. He had to put every item of clothing, including his own underpants and T shirt, into a bucket his mother filled with boiling water and half a packet of detergent. She swirled the clothes vigorously with the mop handle and then told Edwin to drop the sandals into the bucket too, for good measure. The bucket was deposited yards away from the house.

Edwin didn't actually care what happened to Lanthorne's clothes. They could be used for next year's Guy Fawkes dummy or to wipe grease from the car engine. He would never be able to return them to Lanthorne, anyway, because he was never going back to that world. Sometime tomorrow he would need to concoct a story which explained why his friend could no longer be contacted and why it was impossible to get his own clothes back.

Edwin went up to the bathroom and enjoyed the longest soak of his entire life. He used so much of his mother's bubble bath that he disappeared under several feet of foam. Everything about the bathroom was wonderful. It was bright and scented and CLEAN.

Although Edwin was eventually snow-white on the outside, the smell of Jugge's putrid food still clung to the inside of his nose. He tried inhaling the rose-scented bubbles, which simply made him sneeze and didn't wash away the smell. He was desperately hungry, but he wasn't sure when he would be able to face food again.

Mrs Robbins knocked on the bathroom door and asked, "Is the senior SAS operative ready for his dinner?"

"Not sure I'm hungry."

"I can offer you something better than bark and insects."

If only she knew how queasy that remark made him feel.

When Edwin came downstairs, he was pleased to find that hunger was stronger than queasiness, although the custard with the apple pie was a step too far. It might have been hot and rich with vanilla, but its runniness was a horrible reminder of the unspeakable pools into which many of Jugge's items of food had decayed.

Edwin felt dog-tired. After one of his many yawns, his father joked, "You'll need a bit more stamina before the SAS sign you up to save the country."

"They're thinking of sending me to a parallel universe," Edwin joked back and wished he hadn't, because those few words reminded him of how much he never wanted to have anything more to do with Lanthorne's world.

A good night's sleep might make it all disappear, like one of those busy and detailed dreams that dissolve for ever only minutes after you wake up. Edwin was sound asleep by nine o'clock, something unheard of in a school holiday, but such peace of mind was not to last.

The night was blustery and all its sounds could be explained by the wind being up to its usual tricks. Swishing noises were branches struggling as they were wrenched this way and that. Bangs were gates protesting at how poorly they had been fastened, and the wind even seemed to sneak indoors, causing Edwin's bedroom door to swing open and close softly. A breath of night air blew across his cheek and through his hair with the light touch of careful fingers. Edwin was lulled by it all, until the moment Mrs Robbins shrieked, "Someone's taken Mandoline!"

The shriek dragged Edwin from his sleep, but he didn't straight away understand what his mother was saying. It was only when she burst into his bedroom and shouted, "Is Mandoline with you?" that he realized what had happened.

"What do you mean, Mum? No, I..." he struggled to reply.

Mandoline gone? At six months old, she obviously wasn't strong enough to climb out of her cot and wander down to the kitchen for a midnight snack.

Mrs Robbins ran back into her own room shouting, "Ed hasn't got her," while Edwin stumbled out of bed rubbing his eyes.

Next Mr Robbins called out, "Oh Christ, it smells as if a tramp's been in here," and shot downstairs.

Edwin came out onto the landing, not sure what to do or where to go. It was the middle of the night, and his head was still fuzzy.

Mrs Robbins was hovering uncertainly in the doorway of her bedroom, crying. "If I wake up during the night, I *always* check on Mandoline," she mumbled. "But she wasn't there. Edwin, who could have taken her?" She wrapped her arms around herself, gripping the sleeves of her nightie tightly.

Mr Robbins rushed back upstairs, his face so wretched it made Edwin gasp. He was speaking into his mobile phone, jumbling the information he was giving the police with words directed to his son: "The kitchen window's open. No, I haven't touched it. What do you mean 'signs of violence'? Edwin, get dressed NOW. My son and I are going to help you search for her. Surely you can get here sooner than that. EDWIN, what did I just say?"

Edwin returned to his bedroom to put on some outdoor clothes. As he was fastening his jeans, someone began to pound on the back door and he heard his father hurtling downstairs for a second time.

Very soon the house echoed to Mr Robbins's angry voice asking, "What the hell do you want?" There was a pause as whoever had been banging on the door muttered something, and then Mr Robbins yelled, "Edwin, get down here!"

Still only half-dressed, Edwin hurried downstairs, his mother following.

When they entered the kitchen, Edwin's father had his back to them, hiding the short figure who had come in from outside.

"Where did she go? Why didn't you try and stop her?" Mr Robbins demanded. His voice was loud and sharp, and the movements of his arms were threatening.

Edwin peeped around his father. "Lanthorne!"

The grey boy looked even smaller and frailer than before with Mr Robbins looming over him. The bright lights in the kitchen were making his eyes water in streams.

"This is my new friend, Lanthorne," said Edwin. "What's happened, Dad?"

Mr Robbins stepped away and took a deep breath. "He says he saw a woman carrying a shiny baby. What I want to know is what was he doing in our garden at three o'clock in the morning?"

With the three members of the Robbins family now staring expectantly at him, Lanthorne stared back, his eyes very wide. He pulled his hood down against the light and was clearly thinking of running out of the door. Mr Robbins nudged him to one side, locked the door and kept hold of the key. Lanthorne shrank away, as if he was about to be struck.

He said, in a quiet voice, "I needed to see Edwin. She came through the door after him."

Edwin's head was swirling with thoughts and emotions. Mandoline had disappeared and Lanthorne had appeared unexpectedly. A woman had been seen with a shiny baby. How much of this would his parents believe?

"Lanthorne looked after me," he said.

"Well, he's our key witness, and a very peculiar one. Unless it's an act and he's part of some kidnapping plot. Are you?"

Lanthorne jumped back a couple of paces and blinked. "I was trying to help," he replied in an almost inaudible voice. "You're very frightening."

"I'll take Lanthorne upstairs while I finish getting dressed," Edwin told his parents. He and Lanthorne urgently needed to talk.

"I need to get some clothes on as well," said Mr Robbins. With all his running about and phoning, he hadn't had time to change out of his pyjamas.

Mrs Robbins, who had been too upset to join in the conversation, slumped onto a chair. "Why aren't the police here?" she asked her husband. "Did you give them our address?"

As the two boys entered his bedroom, Edwin heard his father say, "I'm still suspicious of that so-called friend."

Edwin shut the door and turned to face Lanthorne. "Auntie Necra's kidnapped my sister, hasn't she?"

With shielded eyes, his grey friend was gawping at the softness and comfort of Edwin's bedroom. He gave a little bounce on the bed where Edwin had seated him.

"Lanthorne!"

"She followed you through the same door, and I followed her. But you didn't see her and she didn't see me. She hid in your garden for hours, until all the lights went out and for a long time after that. I was watching her all the time, but I didn't know she was going to steal your sister, I promise. I thought she was just curious. She's always been interested in Shiners. I thought she'd walk around your home, looking at things, helping herself to the objects she liked. That's what she does in our house when my dad's not there. Then she came out again, holding a shiny baby."

"Mandoline."

"When I told her to put the baby back, she pushed me over. I tried, I really did, but her hands are like rock. I fell down and I was dizzy for ages. After my head cleared, I started banging on your door."

Edwin picked out a thick jumper and some shoes. "She's a monster."

He paused to calm his breathing. The thought of a tiny baby in the clutches of someone like Auntie Necra was very difficult to deal with.

"Once the police arrive, we'll need to explain every-thing," he told Lanthorne. "But what if they don't believe us?"

"What are the 'police'? Do they look after babies?"

"They help find missing people and lock us up if we break the law."

"We have Lawkeepers too. You won't let them hurt me?"

"Of course they won't hurt you. You're their key witness, not a criminal. You'll have to guide the police when they cross into your world to get Mandoline back."

Lanthorne shrank into his hood. He said in a tiny, nervous voice, "I don't think I can do that, Edwin."

Edwin waved the shoe he had just picked up. "You can't refuse to help us, Lanthorne. She's my sister!"

"It's not me, Edwin. It's the doors. You know Jugge said they were *cap*... that word?"

"What about that word? What do you mean?"

"I don't think the doors ever let Lawkeepers through, even in the olden days when your people were chasing after us."

"They let three of us through tonight!"

"Jugge believes that when they get a chance they can be *mali*... that other word."

"Malicious. Will they let us two back, do you think?"

"They know us now. I think they might. I'm so sorry, Edwin. It's my fault Auntie Necra stole your sister."

"How can it be your fault?" Edwin asked roughly. "I was the one who wrote all those childish letters and said I hated my sister. And I obviously didn't shut the door behind me."

Suddenly Lanthorne doubled over and began to sob loudly.

"I've already said it's not your fault," Edwin shouted.

Lanthorne sat up again and put his fists inside his hood, so that he could wipe his eyes. "I don't want to be stuck in your world," he said. "Its brightness is really hurting me. What if Auntie Necra shut the door and locked us out?"

Edwin went very cold. A kidnapper was bound to take precautions to ensure she wasn't followed. Perhaps she was too excited to be careful. "We've got to hope the door remembers you and is staying open until you go back," he said. "Do you really think it's up to *us*?"

Lanthorne nodded.

Edwin was trying to make himself feel brave, but his determination was seeping away by the second. "If it turns out that other people can go through too, I'm definitely coming back for my dad," he said. "He'll pulverize your Auntie Necra when he catches up with her."

"Is that a bad thing?" Lanthorne asked.

"It means there won't be much left of her." Edwin took a deep breath and picked up the backpack lying beside his desk. "Come on, Lanthorne," he said without enthusiasm. "Time to leave my world behind. If we can."

Lanthorne jumped off the bed and joined Edwin by the bedroom door.

"The plan is we sneak out of the back door. I need to get my anorak from the hall and then grab a few things from the kitchen first, though."

Mr and Mrs Robbins were standing outside their open front door, looking for the arrival of the police. Mr Robbins had put on a tracksuit so he was ready to help them search for his daughter. Mrs Robbins was beside him in a dressing gown, crying onto his shoulder. Edwin and Lanthorne crept downstairs into the kitchen unnoticed.

"You wait outside," Edwin said.

"I can't get out, Edwin. He locked the door."

"The window's still half open. Climb up on the cabinet and jump through. Auntie Necra managed it with a baby." *Dad's going to hate himself for not mending the broken catch.*

Lanthorne was quickly out in the darkness, waiting, as Edwin scrabbled about in the kitchen, filling his backpack with anything he thought might come in useful if you were trying to rescue a kidnapped baby.

"That'll have to do," Edwin said as he also clambered out of the kitchen window. Once they heard the police cars arrive and Mrs and Mrs Robbins invite the officers in, the boys slipped down the side of the house.

"We've got about a minute," said Edwin. "They'll call us downstairs, then come looking for us when we don't reply." He led Lanthorne towards a patch of grass, which would deaden their footsteps. Alert neighbourhood dogs were already barking themselves hoarse because the police had used their sirens. Dog owners would soon be up from their beds and looking out of their windows to catch the excitement, so the boys needed to be out of sight straight away. They ran across the grass and into the deep shade of a clump of trees between Grindling Close and the edge of the nearby school playing field. Edwin didn't dare run along lit streets to the allotment, but he had never been too comfortable in the dark. He was no track athlete, and Lanthorne less so, so it wasn't long before each boy had a stitch in his side, but there were overwhelming reasons not to rest.

"I can't see where I'm going, and Dad's calling for me," Edwin managed to gasp as they hurried along.

Lanthorne put his arm through Edwin's, which made running even more difficult.

"We're the only ones who can rescue her, Edwin. I'm sure of it. Come on. Not far now. I'm very good at finding my way in the dark."

8

Know Your Friends

When they reached the right patch on the allotment, the shed door was still partly open and they scrambled gratefully through. For a moment there was the light of Edwin's world behind them—well, not exactly light, but less darkness than the pitch-black emptiness which lay ahead. Edwin was still thinking about going back for his father—and for the police too, despite what Lanthorne had said about the attitude of the doors to the Lawkeepers—but then the door of the allotment shed slammed shut with tremendous violence, and all contact with his own world was snuffed out.

He turned round and extended his hand, anxious to know that the door was still there. His fingers were now the only source of light, five disembodied faintly glowing rods two feet from his body. They found nothing to touch.

Edwin half expected his hand to float away and leave him completely at the mercy of the darkness. It was the deepest darkness he had ever known. Although the soles of his shoes were clearly resting on a rough surface, he had a horrible and growing sense of floating in the blackness, with no idea of direction or up and down. He felt he could easily have been in the depths of outer space, lost for all eternity in the nothingness where stars and planets can never form. Edwin began to feel sick, and he might have collapsed if he hadn't suddenly focused on the sound of Lanthorne breathing heavily beside him.

Edwin turned on his friend, angrily barking his words at the point in the darkness where Lanthorne's head was most likely to be. "Why did you slam the shed door? I was planning to take Mandoline back through it."

"It closed itself," Lanthorne replied. "I expected it would. I think we're in the yard behind Jugge's house."

Edwin desperately wanted to hear him say, *We'll soon find your sister and a door to take her through. Don't worry.* But "Jugge might know what to do," was the best he got.

Might? Jugge *might* be able to help them find his baby sister, the sister he had kept saying he never wanted. Edwin closed his eyes and immediately opened them again as the sensation of floating almost overwhelmed him.

"We need to go inside," he said. "Can you see Jugge's back door?"

"Just about."

Lanthorne took hold of Edwin's sleeve and pulled him across the yard. He sniggered when Edwin banged his nose on the door he couldn't see. The snigger turned into a gasp as Edwin fumbled for the door handle, found it, shook it, couldn't turn it and then started shouting.

"Jugge, we're back. Let us in. Let us in. Jugge!"

"Edwin, don't. Auntie Necra could still be—"

"Still be here? I'll show her!"

Edwin was now kicking the door as well as beating it with his fists. He shouted so loudly it hurt the back of his throat.

In a normal world, when someone opens a door and looks out into the night he is silhouetted by the brightness escaping. This wasn't a normal house in a normal world. When Jugge eventually opened his back door, all Edwin was aware of was a shift from pitch darkness to near-black grey, and an unidentifiable shape leaning towards him.

The shape said, "You two again," in an irritable voice Edwin recognized. It definitely wasn't a *Pleased to see you again. Drop in any time you're passing* kind of voice, and Edwin even thought Jugge might shut the door against them. He couldn't allow that. He shoulder-barged Jugge and rushed past him into the kitchen, before blundering down the passage and into Jugge's main room. If he found Auntie Necra, he wasn't sure what he would do to her once he had snatched Mandoline back. The room was in darkness, so Edwin flailed about with his arms in case Auntie Necra was standing very still and holding her breath somewhere near him. He knew there was a danger that one of his flapping arms might smack Mandoline, but he was desperate. Inevitably, he crashed into a piece of furniture and, as it toppled over, so did he.

"I was in bed," Jugge said in a resentful voice, when he and Lanthorne entered the main room together. Edwin was still lying on the floor. There was a brief silence as Jugge created a spark from somewhere and lit a dirty end of candle. He placed it on a high shelf.

Edwin hadn't really expected Auntie Necra to be there and he could now see that she wasn't. He sat up and stared miserably into the fireplace. Jugge had dampened down the fire for the night and Edwin knew exactly how it felt.

Lanthorne found his usual chair and curled up there without saying a word.

"Lanthorne's Auntie Necra stole my baby sister Mandoline," Edwin said loudly. He got up and dropped heavily into a chair.

"And you've just knocked over my best table for no reason," replied Jugge.

He lit two more dim candles, moving slowly and deliberately as he placed them about the room. He also stood the table up again, with an irritated sigh.

Edwin could see now that Jugge's unusual outline was explained by the length of dull brown cloth he had wrapped around him. It might have been his idea of a dressing gown or simply a blanket off his bed. His bare toes were long and thin and almost as twitchy as the fingers he was using to stop the brown cloth falling down. His neck and head, with its stiff hair, sprouted from the blanket like a grey carrot with a topknot. Jugge's eyes were expressionless black beads. Was he really the only person Lanthorne could have chosen as a best friend?

"You obviously don't care what's happened," said Edwin, not sure whether to scream at Jugge or to appeal to his softer side, just in case he had one.

"I'm trying to think," replied Jugge. He sat down and spent some time arranging the brown cloth so that it covered as much of him as possible, including the twitchy toes. Edwin was glad to see them disappear. "I can't do my best thinking with a not-very-old Shiner snapping at me like a jiggle. You need to calm down, Edwin, while we come up with a plan."

Edwin started messing with the zip on his backpack.

"Did Auntie Necra come back here with the baby?" Lanthorne asked.

"That's one of several possibilities," said Jugge.

"Don't you know?" Edwin snapped.

"I heard doors opening and shutting, which could have been her. Or it could have been some other nighttime event I'd rather not know about."

"If we heard mysterious noises in our house in the middle of the night," Edwin told him contemptuously, "my dad would turn on every single light, call the police and rush downstairs with a couple of golf clubs. All at the same time."

"That's not how it works here, Edwin," said Lanthorne. "If there's a strange noise in the middle of the night, we quietly lock the bedroom door and hide under the bed. It's the safest way. My mum once stayed under her bed for three days, when she heard hissing she didn't recognize."

"All the time we sit here talking and doing nothing, your evil Auntie Necra's getting further and further away with my sister."

"Haven't you got another sister?" Jugge asked.

Edwin's eyes widened with outrage that Jugge had just said this. He sounded as if he thought it was normal for parents to keep spare children handy in case of accidents like kidnapping. He needed shaking up.

Edwin pulled his hand out of his backpack. He was now clutching the small cylindrical object he had been rummaging for. Taking the cushion from the back of his chair, he held it out in front of him. The flame on the lighter he had taken from his parents' kitchen was flicked into life. Lanthorne squealed.

"Starting with this cushion, I'm going to set fire to everything in your house, unless you help me find my sister." Edwin could hardly believe he was threatening an adult in this way. "You're treating it like an everyday thing. It's not. It'll kill my parents if we don't find her."

"Put out the flame," said Jugge. "I've got an idea."

"Let's hear the idea first." Edwin held the lighter closer to the cushion.

Lanthorne shrank into his hood, away from the small, pointed flame.

The two black beads of Jugge's eyes were completely fixed on Edwin, who wasn't sure how long he could hold his threatening pose or what he would do if the cushion actually went up in flames.

"Nothing in our world burns that easily," said Jugge smoothly. "Stands to reason, doesn't it? We hate bright flames, so we're not going to allow our houses to be full of things that catch fire."

This made sense and Edwin extinguished the lighter and dropped it back into his backpack.

"My idea is the obvious one and the best," Jugge announced. "We hand the problem over to Lanthorne's parents to sort out. His mum is Necra's sister, after all."

"No!" said Lanthorne. "They can't be trusted. My mum always argues with Auntie Necra and then does exactly what she says. And my dad's no use because all he ever says is, 'It's nothing to do with me.'"

"That's a stinking idea," said Edwin. "Where's she gone? We have to follow her."

"We know exactly where she's gone," said Jugge.

Edwin couldn't believe how matter-of-factly Jugge told him this. "Where?" he demanded.

"She's gone Out There."

"What do you mean? Out *where*?" Why couldn't these people explain themselves clearly? Did Jugge mean out to sea, out to lunch—or in outer space, even?

"*Out There*," said Jugge, "is a long, long way from here. It's a place where people like Lanthorne and me don't like to go."

"Why?"

Jugge sighed. "Because it's too dangerous."

Edwin fumed. Too dangerous for Jugge, but quite all right for a six-month-old baby? "Why is it dangerous, Jugge?"

"Some of the people Out There are old-fashioned, shall we say." Jugge fiddled with his brown cloth as if the subject were too boring and all he wanted to do was to go back to bed.

"Why are you being so mysterious? This isn't a guessing game. Tell me!"

"You tell him, Lanthorne."

Lanthorne fidgeted on his chair, scratched his arm and decided to tell his story facing the wall. Then he coughed and swallowed as he tried to find the best words.

"We live in the important town of Landarn," Lanthorne began. "There are other people who live Out There. Out There is a long way away, thank goodness. Sort of north. Auntie Necra was born in Landarn like the rest of our family, but when she was young she went to stay with some cousins in the village of Morting."

"Morting is a village in the middle of Out There," interrupted Jugge. "The visit had an effect on her, didn't it, Lanthorne?"

Lanthorne squirmed and scratched his other arm vigorously. He was getting to the main part of what he needed to tell Edwin.

"You see, Edwin, Auntie Necra likes the old-fashioned ways in Morting, the things we used to do ages ago but don't do any more. The things we *ate.*" His voice dropped to almost nothing as he said the last word, and it barely registered with Edwin. "When she insists on coming to stay with us, she keeps going on about our birthright. Mum and Dad say no, no, no, but she won't give up. Swarme..." His voice faltered.

Jugge picked up the story. "His older brother, Swarme, went back to Morting with Auntie Necra, four years ago."

"Auntie Necra says he's very happy there," Lanthorne continued. "Mum would love to go and fetch him back, but Dad says it's not safe. All kinds of nasty things on the road and in the trees."

"That's a good version of the story, Lanthorne," said Jugge, giving him a long look. "Edwin knows all he needs to know."

Edwin could feel that Jugge wanted the incident to end there. A baby had been kidnapped and taken to a dangerous place where no one cared to go. There was nothing to be done. Case closed. End of story. But Edwin couldn't let it end now, with Mandoline out there amongst things probably far worse than any he could imagine. "So you think Auntie Necra's taken Mandoline with her back to Morting?" he said firmly.

"I just said so," Jugge replied.

"We have to get a search party together." Edwin's voice rose in volume with each word. "Nobody likes babies being kidnapped. Why don't you tell your Lawkeepers what Auntie Necra's done?"

"Stop being so bossy, Edwin," said Lanthorne, who hated it when people started shouting. "Jugge's older than us."

"Thank you, Lanthorne," said Jugge. "First of all, Lawkeepers stay away from Out There. They're not daft. Secondly, if I take a Shiner along to see them, they'll lock you up and study you. That won't help your sister."

"Jugge's right," Lanthorne added quietly.

Edwin turned on him. "It's my sister who's been taken. My BABY sister! We're not at school now, being ever so polite to grown-ups and doing exactly what we're told! I know, why don't we send you up the chimney, like one of your stupid letters? We could post you express to Necra's house, and you'll be waiting for her when she arrives. You just recapture Mandoline and jump into the fireplace and you'll be back here in no time."

There was an awkward moment's silence, as Edwin fought to regain his temper.

"That's not a bad idea," said Jugge.

Edwin suspected he was being mocked, but he couldn't be sure.

"I've never heard of actual people being sent that way," Jugge continued. "I'm better than most when it comes to managing chimneys. You'd have to screw yourself up extra small, Lanthorne."

Lanthorne ran to the most shadowy corner of the room.

"I might get lost for ever up there," he sniffed. "I might get cooked!"

"We'll need a bigger fire than usual," Jugge said. "Lots of really efficient smoke."

Edwin couldn't believe his ears. His suggestion was no more than a moment's lashing out in frustration.

He didn't want to see Lanthorne whooshing up the chimney. And as for Jugge, he obviously intended to avoid any risk to himself. So much for all his talk about being modern, and wearing that ridiculous tank top.

"Lanthorne is *not* going up any chimney and that's that," said Edwin. "He's coming with us to find Mandoline."

Jugge stood up, gathered the brown cloth around him and suddenly left the room.

"If he's going to lock his bedroom door and sneak under the bed, I'll set fire to his furniture. I really will!" Edwin shouted after Jugge. "I'll set fire to the whole town if I have to."

Lanthorne returned from the far corner of the room and rested his hand on Edwin's shoulder. "Thank you for not sending me up the chimney, Edwin. If it means we have to go Out There, I won't let you down."

"Jugge's going to let us down, Lanthorne. I can feel it."

They remained in silence for about five minutes, lost in their own thoughts, and just as Edwin had decided they would have to go and find Jugge, the man re-appeared. He now held himself very upright and looked purposeful, as if he had made an important decision. Jugge was dressed in a long, dark coat with a hood which at present was down. In his hand were a second hooded coat and a pair of gloves, Swarme's clothes that Edwin had thrown at him on his last visit.

"Put this coat on over that other thing," Jugge said in a brisk voice, meaning Edwin's anorak. "It's a giveaway. We can't do anything about the shoes. I'm not letting you have any of mine."

"They're proper shoes," said Edwin. He demonstrated by stamping loudly on the floor. Jugge was unimpressed.

"When we get outside, don't speak a word and don't play up," Jugge told him. "I'm beginning to regret I ever took an interest in Shiners."

Lanthorne helped Edwin on with the coat and took the opportunity to whisper, "Behave yourself."

So Jugge had decided to help them, and they were about to take the first steps towards finding Mandoline. Edwin felt a glow of relief spread through his body, but it was also uncomfortable wearing two coats over his thickest jumper.

They left the house with Jugge carrying a single lanthorne to guide their way. Edwin felt as if he were stepping into a bottle of black ink. He took a firm grip of Lanthorne's hand and allowed himself to be led.

They trotted down street after street, although Edwin could barely distinguish street corners or buildings. Their destination was reached after about twenty minutes. All Edwin could make out was a set of tall gates, as Jugge walked past them with the lanthorne, and then a small door where Jugge stopped and knocked gently.

"It's a nagge-yard, I think," said Lanthorne carefully, timing his words so they were covered by the sound of Jugge's knocking.

The proprietor of the building made Jugge look positively handsome by comparison. He was older, taller, thicker set and harder in every way—from his bony fingers to his sharp stare and *I'm only telling you once* voice. Edwin knew as soon as he caught his first glimpse of the man that it would be a grave mistake to answer back. They were grudgingly allowed in.

"This is Trunke," said Jugge. "He might be willing to help."

Trunke's eyes and cheeks were unnaturally sunken, as if he had sucked in impossibly hard. They looked ready to pop back out again at any moment. His skin was grey-tinged, of course, with blotches of yellow that even managed to invade the dark line of his lips. He had been working late and was still wearing a heavily soiled wrap-around leather apron.

"Wait here and don't move," said Trunke. He didn't bother to look at the boys when he said this.

They were left in a lightless corridor, while Trunke and Jugge moved deeper into the house, taking the lanthorne with them. They had been forbidden to move, but not to talk.

"I don't like Trunke at all," said Edwin, as soon as he thought the men were out of earshot.

"We still have Jugge."

"So you say."

"He needn't have helped us at all."

"I suppose so."

"Please don't be cheeky to them, Edwin, now that we might be on the way."

"I don't expect anyone cheeks Trunke."

"Not even his nagges."

"What's a nagge?"

Lanthorne thought for a moment. "They pull our hansommes when we need to travel a long way."

"Like our horses."

"That's a funny sounding name for an animal. *Horses*. Do they get sore throats?"

Edwin couldn't help giggling at this remark.

"Nagges have got a nasty bite."

"I expect Trunke bites them back."

Now it was Lanthorne's turn to giggle.

The door at the end of the corridor opened.

"Come here, you two." This was Trunke and they obeyed at once.

Edwin peeped from under his large hood. He couldn't tell whether they were in a store room or perhaps Trunke's lounge. It lacked even the modest comfort of Jugge's home, having no fire and no furniture other than the two rough chairs on which the men were now sitting. Edwin and Lanthorne remained standing beside the door with their backs to the wall, looking as if they were suspects about to be interrogated. Jugge's lanthorne was on the floor and its light hardly reached anyone's face.

"So this is the Shiner. Let's have a look at him, then," said Trunke in a tone which flattened quite a lot of the hope which had been building inside Edwin.

Edwin didn't know what he was expected to do— walk up to Trunke, offer to shake his hand, say a few words about himself?

"Take off your hood and be quick about it," said Jugge. "Trunke hasn't got all night."

Lanthorne looked at Jugge in surprise. He'd never heard his friend speak as unpleasantly as this to anyone before. Trunke's personality was obviously catching, or perhaps Jugge was as nervous as they were and wanted to create a good impression.

When Edwin was standing bareheaded, and glowing, Trunke said, "I see what you mean. Unnatural, isn't it? Are you sure he won't burn us all to death?" He laughed briefly at his own joke while continuing to stare at Edwin as if he were a freak of Nature with an assortment of extra limbs or tails. When he had stared his fill, he said, "That's enough of that. Put your hood back."

Edwin was too daunted by the man to offer any cheek or to say what he was thinking, which was that if anyone deserved to be stared at it was Trunke himself. He searched for his humblest voice.

"Lanthorne's Auntie Necra has kidnapped my baby sister. Please, are you going to help us?"

Trunke didn't even look at him, let alone answer his question. Jugge answered for him. "Trunke has agreed to drive you along the road to Morting, until..."

"Until he doesn't care to drive you any longer," finished Trunke. "I heard another hansomme go by in that direction, a few hours ago. Rattling along it was, which is unusual at night. Must have been her."

Edwin's heart leapt.

"Thank you so much, Mister Trunke," he said. "Thank you too, Jugge, for coming with us."

Jugge chortled loudly. "Oh I'm not coming with you. You'll never catch me Out There. If I were you, I'd give up and go home. You have no idea."

"Jugge!" Lanthorne's voice was choked with disappointment. "We're only boys. We need your help."

"Make up your minds," said Trunke harshly. "Are you going or staying?"

"I'll go wherever I have to go," said Edwin. He could feel his body trembling as much as his voice. "Lanthorne, you needn't—"

"I'm going wherever Edwin goes," said Lanthorne.

"I've paid Trunke for his trouble," said Jugge. "And here's some money for each of you." He handed each boy a purse, a small leather bag closed by a drawstring. They pocketed them. "So don't accuse me of not helping you. I'm just not big on self-sacrifice. I'll think of something to tell Lanthorne's parents, and I'll keep a fire burning in case you find a way of sending me a letter."

"When you visit my parents, I think you should let my snarghe go, if Auntie Necra hasn't done something to it already," said Lanthorne, suddenly remembering his pet.

"Your what!"

"I caught a snarghe and put it in the cupboard in my bedroom."

Jugge let out a sigh of disbelief.

"It licked me," said Edwin. "Twice."

"Getting the taste of you for later," Trunke added tactlessly.

"Throw it something to eat before you go near it," continued Lanthorne helpfully. "Just in case."

Trunke slapped his leg and shook with laughter. "Last call for Morting," he said. "One last chance to say no!"

Edwin hated Trunke for the mockery in his voice. "You can't put me off," he said.

"Remember that old customs die hard Out There," said Jugge, suddenly much more serious. "Let's hope you don't come across them."

9

On the Road

"Do exactly what Trunke tells you," said Jugge. "He knows what's what. I'm off now. So long."

And that was his goodbye. Lanthorne stared at the door for some moments after Jugge closed it behind him. Edwin could tell how let down he felt.

Trunke left them without a light, saying he had to "make preparations." When he returned an hour later, he had to shake both boys awake.

"Do you want to go or not?" he asked irritably, as they shuffled behind him into the stable attached to his house.

It had none of the reassuring smell of straw and solid, friendly horses and their business that Edwin would have expected in a stable at home. The smell here was an acrid stink that made his eyes water as soon as he stepped inside. It woke him up.

"Don't ever look a nagge directly in the eye," Trunke told the boys. "It gives them ideas. I'm taking one of the private hansommes, which means you won't be seen. Now get in, the pair of you."

He was in his travelling clothes: thick, shapeless trousers and a hooded leather jacket that resembled a small tent. His crude boots had hobnails which made scratching sounds on the stable floor.

Narrow steps were set just in front of the right-hand wheel of the hansomme. Trunke pushed the boys up and into the two-person passenger seat. For a moment, before he was forcibly made to sit down, Edwin was able to look along the shafts and at the strange animal between them. A nagge wasn't a horse exactly—or a cow, or a lizard. It had elements of all three, as if an ugly horse had swallowed a lizard and then put on a cow suit. Hip bones and ribs were visible beneath skin that had the colour and texture of a lichen-covered tombstone.

"How long will it take us to get to Morting?" Edwin asked.

"As long as it takes and perhaps a bit longer," Trunke barked.

With a flick of his wrist, he pulled a series of hinged flaps down and across the front of the hansomme, then locked them in place. The boys sat in shocked silence, listening to a key turn twice. This was followed by a prolonged, wheezy, rasping sound and then a particularly loud snap that echoed in the small space in which they were confined. Then they fell backwards in their seat as the hansomme began to move. Edwin hated being shut up in a box. He banged on the flaps, which fitted so tightly together they didn't even rattle.

"I'm making sure you're safe. Keep quiet!"

Edwin nursed his hand. He had skinned several knuckles.

"Trunke's right, Edwin. No one can hurt us in here, and no one can see you shining."

Lanthorne snuggled down and sighed. It was a comfortable sigh, a *Believe it or not, I'm quite looking forward to this adventure* kind of sigh. Edwin snorted and pressed his face into his hood and prepared to be very miserable. He was trying hard not to think that the passenger box of a hansomme resembled a coffin.

Eventually he did fall into a half-doze, which was spoilt by Lanthorne poking him and saying, "Edwin, I'm thirsty. Have you got any of those fizzy cans in your pack?"

"I've brought two. If we drink them now, we'll end up having to wee in here or burst. Let's wait until we stop."

"I'm really, really thirsty."

"Wait!"

They settled back into their respective dozes. There was a half-smile on Lanthorne's lips, but Edwin twitched uneasily from time to time.

Finally, the hansomme came to a stop. Trunke folded back the flaps and said, "Short rest."

The cleaner air and daylight were very welcome even though, to Edwin, the air had a mouldy edge to it and the daylight was very subdued.

The boys climbed down from the hansomme and took in their surroundings. Well, they were certainly on a country road and a long way from Landarn. The road had a scruffy verge on either side and then the hedges started—tall, dark, thorny and overhanging the road as if they intended to meet and make a tunnel. It wasn't the location you would choose for a pleasant country drive. Lanthorne was far more taken with it than Edwin.

"So many trees and bushes," he said. "It's like a giant garden."

Edwin rolled his eyes. He remembered autumn and winter walks in the countryside with his parents; clean, sharp air to breathe and multicoloured leaves to scuff underfoot. Here, there was a strong sense of permanent dampness, of vegetation rotting as soon as it put out leaves, and of mildew clinging to it. The relief of being outside began to wear off. He looked up at the heavy sky, dirty as a puddle. The sun, barely visible, reminded him of a watery blister you didn't dare burst.

Edwin looked at his watch. *Noon.* How many hours, or even days, of travelling were left? He would have felt more comfortable if Trunke had told them how long the journey was likely to last. One fewer unknown to worry about. His staring at the watch drew Trunke's attention.

"Better I take care of that horlogge."

Edwin didn't understand.

"He means the horlogge on your arm," said Lanthorne. "It's only the third one I've ever seen."

Trunke wanted his watch. Didn't Lanthorne realize "take care of it" meant *steal*? Who cared how many he had seen before?

"I don't know what you're talking about," said Edwin.

"Give me the horlogge. It'll be safer with me."

"Better let Trunke take care of it," said Lanthorne quietly. "You might lose it."

Edwin felt his eyes prickle. At that moment, the nagge turned its head to see what was going on. Edwin looked straight into malevolent, bloodshot yellow eyes and saw its leathery lips retract in what could be taken as a sneer or threat. The beast stamped one of its hoofed feet so heavily all three felt the ground vibrate.

"The nagge's hungry," said Trunke. "She's even more bad-tempered when her belly's empty."

Edwin was reminded that if Trunke took against him and left him by the roadside, he wouldn't survive. The nagge was a domesticated animal yet she looked ready to devour him, so what would one of their wild animals do? Anything wild in this country was bound to enjoy ripping a twelve-year-old Shiner to shreds.

"I expect you're right about the horlogge," Edwin said as unresentfully as he could manage. "You have it for safekeeping. I thought I might be able to use it like a compass, but I don't remember how to do it exactly."

He slid the watch from his wrist and dropped it onto Trunke's outstretched palm.

At least when the battery died Trunke wouldn't be able to replace it.

"You can take the hood right down if you like," said Trunke, as if this made up for robbing Edwin. "We're not expecting visitors. If you brought any food, eat it now."

Trunke appeared to think that Edwin's backpack only contained unripe food he himself would find unpalatable. This suited Edwin, who was careful not to let the backpack jingle or clunk whenever he moved it or put it on. Their present safety and his and Mandoline's escape from this world might depend on what he had managed to throw into the backpack during those few moments in his parents' kitchen. He couldn't have Trunke poking about in it and helping himself to anything that took his fancy.

Edwin squatted down and noiselessly unzipped his bag. He handed Lanthorne a can of lemonade and opened the other for himself.

"Goody. I like this," said Lanthorne.

"He just stole my watch, and all you can say is 'Goody'?"

"He left us the money. He knows we've each got a purse."

"I suppose so."

Trunke led the nagge to the thorn hedge where she tucked into the spiky twigs, crunching them noisily. He returned just when Edwin was taking a box of cheese triangles and some biscuits from his pack.

"What have you got there?"

As the top of the backpack was gaping open, Edwin unobtrusively rezipped it and waved the box of cheese triangles in the air as a distraction. He peeled away the foil wrapping from one of the triangles and held it out for Trunke to inspect.

"It's unripe. Don't be disgusting."

Edwin popped the whole triangle into his mouth and moved it around like the contents of a washing machine.

Trunke pulled a face and looked away.

Edwin was pleased with his small triumph but Lanthorne suddenly put everything at risk.

"It's not just horrible unripe Shiner food that Edwin's got in his pack," he said, with the brightness of a five-year-old who doesn't know he's revealing an important secret. "He's got lots of other really interesting things too. He told me."

"He means I've got these," Edwin said, almost shouting as he waved a packet of biscuits under Trunke's nose.

"No, I mean—"

"You'll like these, Trunke!" Edwin really was shouting now.

"Squashed-fly biscuits," said Lanthorne, who was still not aware of what had happened.

Trunke looked at the biscuits with interest.

"They're actually called Garibaldis," said Edwin.

"That's a long name for flies, dead or alive," said Trunke. "I'll take one."

Edwin handed him half the packet. Trunke nibbled one of the biscuits, decided he liked it and polished off the rest very quickly. "Good quality flies," he said. "At least you lot got something right."

"They're currants," said Edwin firmly.

"Don't you believe it. I know a decent fly when I taste one."

He went back to attend to the nagge.

Edwin was now free to turn on Lanthorne and stun him with the full force of his anger.

"Don't you ever do something as stupid as that again," he hissed.

"I thought you didn't mind sharing your biscuits."

"I'm not talking about the biscuits. I mean telling him there are all those other things in my pack. I'll probably need every single one of them to get home."

Lanthorne realized his mistake and hung his head. "I just wanted him to know how you think of everything." To placate his friend, he put half a cheese triangle in his mouth and pretended to enjoy it. This proved impossible and he spat it out.

"You're too picky," Edwin told him coldly. "You gobble up the biscuits and the lemonade and then waste the cheese by spitting it out. There's no difference."

"Yes, there is a difference," Lanthorne said firmly. "I like sweet things. And in any case, cheese should be green."

It had been a very small breakfast, too fizzy and cheesy, and would probably all come back up again when they started bouncing about once more in the hansomme. Edwin longed for a boiled egg and toast. "How far do you think Morting is?"

"My mum always says, 'Thank goodness Out There is too far away to measure,' which doesn't tell us anything."

"We could ask Trunke to keep the hansomme open for some of the time. I was finding it difficult to breathe."

Lanthorne welcomed the suggestion. "Let's enjoy ourselves looking at the countryside," he said, hoping Edwin's bad temper was passing.

Edwin shrugged. "It'll be fresher," he replied meaningfully. "Stop trying to squash your empty can, and give it to me. At some point we might need to fill these cans with dirt and knock people out with them. I saw it done in a film."

This information meant nothing to Lanthorne, who got up to deal with the effects of drinking so much lemonade. Edwin copied him further down the hedge, and then they climbed back into the hansomme. Trunke agreed to let them ride with the flaps half-open. Edwin was told to keep his face mostly hidden, which he didn't mind because soon both boys began to feel cold. The increasing chill of the afternoon didn't seem to bother Trunke. From time to time he was willing to join in conversation of a straightforward, never really friendly, kind.

"It's thorn trees all the way," he said. "You'll soon get fed up with looking at it."

Edwin's interest was much shorter-lived than Lanthorne's. He began to slump more and more in his seat. As he looked down, he noticed that stowed behind Trunke was a piece of wood the length of a broom handle and tipped with a piece of sharp metal.

"What's this pole for, Trunke?" he asked.

"It's in case."

"In case of what?"

"You know what these woods are like. The nagge can take a big piece out of anything, but I like to have a weapon myself."

"Have you been on this road lots of times before?"

"I might have. I think it's time I closed you down. When it begins to get dark you'll shine like a candle, and we can't have that."

They weren't sorry to be in the shelter of a closed passenger compartment once again, and, against his better judgement, Trunke promised not to lock it.

"I'd love to know what time it is," Edwin said after a while. He hoped Lanthorne felt guilty about going along so readily with the theft of his watch.

"It's late afternoon," said Lanthorne. "And soon it'll be night. I wouldn't want to be out in these woods on my own at night."

It might come to that, when I've recaptured Mandoline, Edwin thought with a shiver, and the prospect was so frightening he needed a change of topic to put it out of his mind.

"Tell me about the olden days," he said. "Why were they so different?"

"Because they weren't the same at all," Lanthorne said vaguely. "People didn't believe what we believe now."

"Like what?"

"You know."

"Why won't you tell me?"

"I need another nap."

"No you don't."

"We could look in our purses."

Edwin allowed himself to be distracted. "All right. Mine first."

He hoped they weren't going to find that Jugge had tricked them with a collection of jingly rubbish. The purse certainly felt as if it contained coins, so he hoped for the best.

Unknotting the strings of the purse proved difficult in the dark. When Edwin had accomplished this and poured a few of the contents into the palm of his hand, he had no idea what they looked like.

"Even I can't see them properly in this dark," Lanthorne said disappointedly. "And if we open a flap, Trunke will know what we're doing. He might take them off us."

Edwin put his hand in his backpack and rummaged about. "*Voilà!* I was saving this for a real emergency."

"What's a *voilà*?"

"This *voilà* is the slimline screwdriver and torch my dad uses when he has to change plugs in the kichen. *Voilà!*"

He switched on the torch and Lanthorne's eyes widened with delight as its narrow beam picked out the coins which lay in the palm of Edwin's hand. They were two shades of brown, yellowish brown and greyish brown, and large and heavy like old-fashioned pennies.

"Ooh," said Lanthorne. "Doubla and florines. We could buy a lot with these."

"Thank you, Jugge," said Edwin. He was very relieved. "What are the pictures on them? Do you have a king or queen's head?"

"These are buildings in Landarn and that's someone important in the Governa. I don't know his name. It's a long time since we had a king or queen. The Governa tell us what to do now. I've never had florines of my own."

Lanthorne's hoard of coins was identical. They had eight coins each.

"What are you up to in there?"

Perhaps Trunke had heard the chink of coins above the clopping of the nagge's hooves. They would have to be very careful what they said, if his hearing were so acute.

"We're playing a guessing game," Edwin called out. "Sorry if we upset the nagge."

"Just watch yourselves."

They silently repocketed the coins. Suddenly the torch went out, although Edwin hadn't switched it off. He shook it and was rewarded with a brief goodbye flicker.

"My dad *never* checks the batteries in things," he said. Just as they started dozing off again, Edwin whispered,

"I haven't forgotten about the olden days." Something told him this would be important knowledge to have in Morting.

"I promise I'll tell you soon, Edwin," Lanthorne replied.

And, for the moment, they left it at that.

10

Lovely Lodgings

Eventually the clip-clopping stopped. Edwin had grown used to the steady bouncing up and down and the occasional crack as a pebble was flicked against the underside of the hansomme. He held his breath as he listened to make sure that the journey to Out There really had come to an end.

"Where are we?" Lanthorne asked, sleepily rubbing his eyes.

Trunke folded back the hansomme flaps.

"Is this Morting?" Edwin asked eagerly.

"That's another day's journey up the road."

Edwin's face fell. *Another day!*

"I've told you I'll get you there, and I will. For now, it's supper and bed." Trunke's manner was less abrupt, if not exactly friendly, which made Edwin think a little better of him.

When the boys stumbled onto the ground beside the hansomme, their legs were so stiff they moved as if they were only just learning to walk.

It was possible to make out the shape of a large building set back from the road. Not a single ray of light escaped from it, which might mean the shutters were tightly closed against things out here in the dark. It might even be a ruin. He thought it would be in character for Trunke to expect them to sleep in a roofless shell of a building. In this country, it was probably impossible to tell what was a home and what was an abandoned dump. Bright lights and a cheerful voice saying, "Come in, your rooms are ready," would have been lovely.

Edwin stood close to Lanthorne in case he lost him in the darkness. Above their heads—in a sky that felt heavy, as if gloominess were an actual thing that draped itself over this whole world—not a single star shone.

"Is this really an inne?" Lanthorne asked excitedly.

If he says it's the first one he's ever stayed in, I shall scream, Edwin thought. *We're not on a school outing.*

"Now listen very carefully," said Trunke, bringing his face to within a few inches of theirs.

Edwin couldn't help flinching. Up close, the man looked even more as if he had just returned from a holiday in the grave.

"This place is dangerous," Trunke said quietly and

slowly. "Not risky, not unsafe. It's very, very *dangerous*. You can never tell who's passing through and what they might like to do to you."

Edwin felt cold fingers grip his stomach. His relief that he'd moved a whole day nearer to finding his sister was swept away by this news.

Trunke prodded him sharply in his chest. "*You* keep quiet and cover every part of yourself, all the time. There's no way I can explain a Shiner out here. Do you understand me?"

"Yes," said Edwin, resenting the prodding finger and wanting to prod Trunke back very hard.

"You'll be sharing a room, but I'll be on my own. I'm not having you shining at me all night long. Now, what are *you* not going to do?" He pushed Edwin backwards with another hard prod.

"Not show any part of me and not speak," Edwin muttered. And to think he believed that Trunke was becoming friendlier. He hadn't disliked anyone so much for a long time. Well, Auntie Necra was miles clear at the top of his unpopularity list, but Trunke was definitely in second place.

"By the way, you two are footing the bill."

He directed the boys towards the door of the inne. "Hand over one of the purses Jugge gave you."

Edwin poked Lanthorne's arm. It was his friend's turn to be robbed. Let him see how he liked it.

138

"Shall I give you three florines?" Lanthorne asked sweetly. It didn't work.

"I'll take the whole purse," said Trunke. And he did.

Once he had pocketed the money, Trunke conducted a quick inspection of both boys. He drew their hoods so far down over their faces they could barely see their shoes and pulled the sleeves of their coats well beyond their wrists, even though Edwin had put Swarme's gloves back on.

"We're still taking a risk with those shoes, though," Trunke said. "Nobody here wears shoes like that."

"They're really old and scruffy," Edwin said. First Jugge and now Trunke going on about a pair of knocked-about shoes. Anyone would think he was wearing those little-girly ones with flashing coloured lights.

As he was about to open the front door, Trunke suddenly blurted out, "What am I thinking of! You can't go inside with that on your back."

He gave Edwin's backpack a heavy slap. It responded with a scrunching sound.

Here we go, thought Edwin. He was prepared to put up a struggle to keep possession of the backpack, but it was a huge disadvantage having it slung behind him.

"You've no right to take it!" Lanthorne squared up to Trunke, putting his hands on his hips and looking like a puppy challenging a bulldog. "It's got his baby sister's toys in it, and I expect you've just broken them all."

Trunke muttered a few sounds that weren't quite words. He wasn't used to being told off by puppies. "I didn't say he couldn't keep it. I said he couldn't wear it on his back. It's too different and it'll draw attention. Those colours."

"Dark burgundy and taupe," said Edwin. He was so glad it wasn't bright yellow and sporting a crazy logo.

"He can carry it in front of him, with his arms wrapped all the way round it. Or leave it in the hansomme."

"I'll carry it," said Edwin.

Their attention was diverted by a loud creak from overhead. Edwin guessed it was the inne sign swinging in a breeze they couldn't feel. He wondered what the inne was called. The Shameless Thief, perhaps?

Once they were inside, Trunke made them stand by the door.

"Stay here," he said, tapping a spot on the floor to show them that "here" meant "exactly here". Then he hurried off.

Neither boy dared utter a word. Edwin clutched the backpack closely to his chest, with his face pressed into the top of it. He was afraid of what might happen if he showed even part of his face by peering around. At the very least, Trunke would probably smack him on the back of the head, but there might be other people who would want to run off with a Shiner, as Auntie Necra was doing with Mandoline.

"Everything's paid for," Trunke said under his breath when he returned holding two small lanthornes. "I've ordered a mixture of ripe and unripe food for you. They think you're my nephews and, if anyone asks, we're going to visit your grandmother, who's too old to move into town." He wouldn't have said all this if there had been other customers nearby to overhear. Edwin's racing heart slowed down.

Trunke pushed them quickly across the main room of the inne, through a door and into a hallway containing a staircase. The boys climbed this with a good deal of stumbling, followed a dog-leg passage to its end and eventually arrived at their small room, tucked well out of the way at the back of the inne.

As soon as he entered the bedroom, Edwin threw back his hood and took off his gloves.

"I didn't say..." Trunke began.

"I don't care," said Edwin. "I was suffocating."

Trunke grunted. "You've got a jar of water over there and you can have one of the lanthornes." He put it down on the table between the two narrow beds. "I expect that door's the toilette room. I'm going to get your food now."

"Mine will be unripe, won't it?" Edwin asked.

"I explained that one of you's a very fussy eater. They laughed out loud and said I should be firmer with you. I won't be long. There's to be no noise and no coming outside or I'll drive straight back to Landarn and leave you."

Edwin sat on the nearest bed, and placed the backpack beside him.

Trunke paused by the door. "Remember what I've told you. And lock up after me."

As they heard his footsteps marching down the passage, the boys at last found something to smile at.

"How did you know what was in here?" Edwin said, pointing to his backpack.

"I didn't know. I guessed. It's what I'd put in my bag if I was trying to find my baby sister."

"Well guessed, you," Edwin told him. "It certainly shut Trunke up."

Lanthorne felt forgiven. He lay full-length on his bed, his hands behind his head. "This is almost as comfortable as my bed at home," he said. "I like this room."

Edwin's eyes widened, but he said nothing. Lying down on his own bed, he could feel the coarseness of the single blanket, and the pillowcase was already chafing the back of his neck. The room was like every other room he had seen in this world—rough walls and floor and furnishings with barely a trace of colour. Did these people realize they were living in sheds? And whatever lurked in the toilette room was making its malodorous presence felt from a distance of ten feet.

Their food was a long time coming.

"Do you think I should open the door and look outside, Edwin?"

"He told us not to."

"He promised he'd be back soon."

What if Trunke was already on his way back to Landarn with a purse full of money and a big grin on his face? "I don't think a tiny peep would hurt," Edwin said.

Lanthorne unlocked the door and opened it a fraction. He moved only just enough of his head through the doorway to give him a one-eyed squint along the passage. After less than a minute, he locked the door again.

"I was hoping he'd left the food outside and forgotten to tell us," he said.

"But he hadn't."

"No."

The cheese triangles began to call to Edwin from his backpack. They were very persuasive.

"What could you see?" he asked Lanthorne.

"I didn't see anything. It's just a passage."

"Oh. I thought there might be colourful paintings on the walls and spotlights and a thick carpet like the one you saw in my bedroom."

Sarcasm was a sure sign that hunger was getting the better of him. He opened the backpack and ate another of the cheese triangles even if it did mean one meal fewer for Mandoline when he escaped with her.

The waiting got longer and hungrier. Edwin looked automatically at the pale spot on his wrist where his watch had once been.

"Why don't I tell you something nice to pass the time?" Lanthorne said.

Edwin didn't imagine there was anything Lanthorne could tell him which he would find in any way "nice".

"All right," he said dully.

"I think my parents are going to give me new shoes and a boxe for Nollig."

"What's Nollig?"

"What's Nollig! Nollig Day's the best day of the year. We give presents and have special food and we visit friends. If we have any. Nollig's in a few days' time. Don't tell me you don't have Nollig?"

"It sounds just like our Christmas," Edwin said. "They're obviously at the same time." The memory of the brightness and joy of past Christmases made his voice tremble.

"I've been dropping hints all year," said Lanthorne.

"Why do you want a box for Nollig?"

"Nollig boxes are special. They have lids with hinges. I'm hoping for one with a lock, so I can put my special possessions in it."

"I keep mine in a box too," said Edwin. "Hidden in a cupboard."

"We hang up bundles of twigs for decoration, and my

mum serves the food we put in the cupboard months ago to ripen."

The "nice" moment faded with the mention of ripe food.

"I want to do something really nasty to Trunke, even if he did let me keep my backpack for the moment," Edwin said, needing to change the subject. "I'd like to run him over with his own hansomme. Backwards and forwards at least three times, and then I'd pick my watch out of the mess."

Lanthorne was also finding his grumbling stomach difficult to cope with. "I'm going down the passage," he announced.

"Is it safe?" Edwin asked. He knew that, deep down, he didn't really care if it was safe or not. They had to be sure what was going on. He pulled his hood right down over his face and put his gloves on again. He waited just inside the doorway as Lanthorne tiptoed to the end of the dim passage and disappeared.

Edwin waited. And waited. He guessed that at least twenty minutes had passed. Surely Lanthorne hadn't run away and left him too? Was this a cruel plan to torment a Shiner for being so, well, shiny? Suddenly there was the sound of heavy footsteps, confident footsteps that didn't care if they were heard. They certainly weren't made by a puny boy like Lanthorne. Edwin was so shocked, he didn't at first think to retract his head, even when the maker of the footsteps turned the corner. A tall figure was framed anonymously in the light from the single lanthorne, and it was approaching with long strides. Edwin came to his senses, pulled his head back in and managed to lock the door.

"Please don't knock. Please don't knock..." he whispered from the far side of his bed, where he was now crouching. The figure knocked, waited and then knocked again loudly.

"What are you playing at in there?" It was Trunke! "*You* shouldn't be the one opening the door," he said in a fierce voice when Edwin let him in. He was carrying a tray and he looked around suspiciously. "Where is he? If he's gone off exploring..."

"He's in the toilette room. We got very hungry while we were *waiting for you*, so I let him have some of my food. It disagreed with him."

"I'm not surprised," said Trunke. "What you lot put in your mouths would give anyone the gripes. This'll have to do for breakfast as well." He set the tray down on Lanthorne's bed. "Lucky for you they had only just put some food away to ripen. It's not what people come here to eat. Be grateful I went to the trouble, and don't leave the room before I call for you in the morning. My room's not far away and I've got the hearing of a throttlebird."

Trunke turned his head towards the toilette-room door. "You in there. Did you hear what I just said?"

146

"Lanthorne's still busy cleaning himself up," Edwin said. "He didn't get there in time."

"That's *your* fault. You should have waited till I came back. You've kept me from my supper long enough." He pointed his finger meaningfully at Edwin and then left.

Edwin sat down beside the tray of food. He wondered whether he should have told Trunke the truth. If Lanthorne were in danger, Trunke could help him, but if Lanthorne weren't in any danger at all and was just nosing about the inne, Trunke was bound to be angry. Knowing Lanthorne as he did, it didn't seem a risk worth taking.

He unbuttoned his coat and started to play nervously with the zip of his anorak, moving it up and down until it snagged and he had to stop. More minutes went by and there was still no sign of Lanthorne. Edwin looked at the spot on his wrist where his watch had been. He needed to think of something else. Food.

On the tray Trunke had brought were a jug of water and two suspiciously stained wooden cups as well as two grey cloths, one at each end, covering ripe and unripe food, Edwin guessed. He slowly lifted a corner of the cloth nearest to him. A wizened nugget of bread came into view. He lifted the cloth a little higher. Now he could see a couple of shrivelled apples and a piece of cheese that resembled a sweating bar of soap. So this must be the unripe supper and breakfast. He had no intention of lifting the other cloth even a fraction. He was very hungry indeed, particularly now there was food of a sort right in front of him, but he didn't think it would be right to tuck in until he knew his friend was safe. He stared at the world's most unappetizing picnic and wondered how long he could hold out before attacking it.

The answer was not very long at all. He ate the bread and apples, but couldn't face the cheese so he slid it under the cloth which covered the rest of Lanthorne's food. He also drank more than half the water straight from the jug, pouring it directly into his mouth. The mugs looked as if they had been used to decant the water from a pond, or worse.

There was a knock at the door, a delicate scrape made by fingers not wanting to draw attention to the sound they made.

"Edwin, it's me."

Edwin hurried to unlock the door.

Lanthorne ran in, unharmed and strangely excited. "I need to calm down," he gasped. "Oh, Edwin, you'll never believe what... Food!" He whisked the remaining cloth from the tray.

It was exactly as Edwin had predicted. What was revealed looked as if it had been fermenting away at the bottom of a dustbin for weeks. On one side of the room, the stink in the toilette room was battering the door to be let out, and now he was presented with the sight and smell of the decomposing version of his own dried-up meal. In the face of brown, squishy apples, bread marbled with streaks of green and cheese too appalling to describe, all Edwin could do was to throw himself onto his bed and bury his face in his pillow. "Eat it quickly," he said. "I think I'm going to die!"

The pillow turned out to be quite an effective gas mask and Edwin hoped that if Lanthorne put all the titbits from hell inside him, the smell would mostly disappear with them.

Eventually there came a gentle tap on Edwin's shoulder. Lanthorne dropped onto the bed beside Edwin, beaming with delight. It was the first time Edwin had seen Lanthorne's tiny discoloured teeth so close up. Unfortunately, they were still smeared with the putrid mush he had been guzzling. Edwin clenched his eyes shut. Concerned for his friend, Lanthorne leant over and brought his face close to Edwin's. He breathed out, making Edwin gasp.

"Get away! Get away RIGHT NOW!"

Confused, Lanthorne went back to his own bed and sat there waiting patiently for Edwin to tell him what he'd done wrong.

"It's not you, Lanthorne. It's your food. Please, please never breathe it over me again."

"Sorry."

"If I have to live on ripe food while I'm here, I won't survive. Nor will Mandoline."

Lanthorne couldn't in all honesty understand why Edwin was making such a fuss. *He* hated unripe food, but you wouldn't catch him screaming at his friends if they ate it in front of him. He was also desperate to tell Edwin what had happened when he went exploring.

"Are you ready for my news?"

"Yes. Go ahead."

Lanthorne jumped up and clapped his hands together. "I've seen Swarme. My brother Swarme! I've seen him. He's here in this inne with us."

11

Strange Meeting

"Where did you see him? What did he say? Can he help us? No, just a minute. Does that mean Auntie Necra's here too? You said Swarme lives with her. Is he helping her to look after Mandoline? She could be nearby."

Lanthorne had settled himself comfortably on the edge of the bed, but Edwin's questions stunned him. For a moment, he couldn't reply. Then he shook his head as if to free it of the idea that Auntie Necra and Mandoline might be under the same roof.

"Trunke would know if she was here with your sister, Edwin. Everybody at the inne would be talking about it. Babies make a lot of noise, don't they?"

"So what's Swarme doing here?"

"I don't know. We've got to find out."

Edwin breathed in and out noisily, to calm himself. What Lanthorne had said made sense. Trunke would have picked up any talk about Auntie Necra turning up at the inne, especially if she was carrying a baby of any kind. She would have wanted to get home to Morting as soon as she could.

"I agree that we have to find Swarme as soon as we can," Edwin said. "He's bound to have important information we can use. Sorry, I interrupted your story."

Lanthorne made himself comfortable again and began. "I saw Swarme, but he didn't see me. That's the first thing. He must be working here. My mother sometimes says, 'I wonder what job our Swarme is doing.' Now I can tell her! I followed the passage all the way back to the staircase, and I even went halfway down."

"That was very daring of you."

Lanthorne smiled at the praise. "At first there was no one about, because I think they were having dinner somewhere. I could hear kitcheny sorts of sounds. Then I heard someone running towards the stairs and I needed a place to hide. I went down the nearest passage and opened a door that looked like a cupboard."

Edwin took in a loud breath.

"It *was* a cupboard."

Edwin relaxed.

"So I shut myself in. I was really frightened because I thought the footsteps were following me. They stopped right in front of where I was hiding, but then the person making the footsteps knocked on a door and a man

152

answered it. The footsteps person said, 'It's ready. If you want some, you need to come right away. We've got some serious eaters in tonight.'"

"What was ready?" Edwin asked.

"Their dinner, I expect. They walked back to the staircase together and I opened the door just a little bit, because I knew the footsteps' voice! When he turned sideways as he was going down the stairs, I could see it really was Swarme. He's taller and a bit fatter now, but it was definitely him."

"It was dangerous opening that door before they'd completely gone."

"I'm glad I did. We've got a friend now, Edwin. Someone on our side, not like Jugge and Trunke. I've got to talk to Swarme. I've just got to."

"Are you sure we'll be able to trust him?"

Lanthorne stared at Edwin. "Of course we can. He's my brother."

"He might not like Shiners."

"You can't help being a Shiner. You're my friend, anyway. That'll be enough for Swarme."

Edwin could feel a plan forming. "Trunke said he wouldn't be back till the morning, so he won't know if we go looking for your brother. The trouble is..."

They didn't know who else was staying at the inne, that was the trouble. But if Lanthorne's brother was happy to work there, surely it couldn't be half as bad as

Trunke made out. It might, despite all Trunke's warnings, be a common or garden, boring old country inne that happened to be set in the middle of nowhere and where nothing unusual happened—other than people treating rotten food as a delicacy.

"I think Trunke's been exaggerating," Edwin said. "He'll be in the bar buying everyone drinks with our money and laughing at us for being so scared. What must we have looked like, walking along with our hoods right down, blind as bats and falling over? He probably wet himself laughing."

"Should we just run downstairs?" Lanthorne asked.

They decided it was still wiser to be careful.

"We need a really good plan," Edwin said.

"Go on, then," said Lanthorne, happy for Edwin to take the lead.

"We've got to sort out the geography, and we need weapons. Good ones."

"You really know how to do this, Edwin," said Lanthorne, hugely impressed. "I didn't bring a weapon, though. Did you?"

"I've got the two lemonade cans but we haven't managed to fill them with dirt yet. Let's see if I've forgotten anything."

He opened his backpack and rummaged.

"The screwdriver-torch and Mum's penknife." He shook the torch but the batteries obviously were completely dead. "I couldn't stab anyone, but I'll put the penknife in my pocket just in case."

He held up the lighter. "I don't mind threatening to set fire to something." The lighter went in his other pocket.

"I'm very good at biting," Lanthorne said.

"Biting it is, then. That can be your weapon. And kicking. And running away. We can both do that."

They turned their thoughts to the floorplan of the building.

"I think we're in one corner of the inne, and it's probably all bedrooms here," Edwin said.

"The stairs are right in the middle," Lanthorne added. "And we know the room where they eat can't be far away, because I heard those noises."

"That's where Trunke will be right now," Edwin said. "He told me he was going to have his supper. Let's hope he spends ages stuffing himself."

"And if Swarme serves the food, we could wait for him out of sight and speak to him when he's on his own." Suddenly Lanthorne clapped his hands together. "What if his room's in this part of the inne? It might even be next door!"

Edwin was doubtful. You never knew what to expect in this world, but he didn't think the inne's staff would sleep in rooms near the guests. "We can't just keep an eye on the passage in case Swarme turns up," he said.

"We're bound to miss him if we do that. We need to go downstairs and actually *find* him."

"I can't wait to see the look on his face," said Lanthorne excitedly. "I won't tell him I gave you his clothes, though."

Or that my mum put them in a bucket of Persil and dumped them in the garden, thought Edwin. He put his gloves back on for the umpteenth time that day.

"Did you come across any other cupboards we could hide in, if we had to?" he asked.

"None I was sure about. What if we opened a door and somebody was there, in bed?"

"Do you think they'd scream if a Shiner suddenly came in, like we scream if we see a ghost?"

"Why do you scream if you see a ghost?"

Edwin wasn't sure how to answer. It seemed to him the obvious thing to do if an apparition stepped through the wall in front of you. "Wouldn't you scream?" he asked.

"It depends if I knew the ghost. Some of them are just plain silly."

Edwin was silent for a long moment. Was Lanthorne suggesting that ghosts regularly popped up all over the place? This was a new thought he couldn't deal with at the moment. He took an extra-firm grip of his backpack and slipped it over his shoulders. "Hoods down," he said.

At least half of him hoped that the first door they opened would be a doorway home, but he also knew he couldn't go through one of those until he had Mandoline safely in his arms. Doors in the inne probably only ever opened into places like the toilette room, in any case.

They crept to the end of the passage outside their room without mishap, and were quickly at the top of the staircase. Here, they had to take the plunge, literally, into near darkness and possibly great danger. Going down was easy for Lanthorne, but Edwin had so much to contend with—a hood, a backpack, near darkness and stairs—that he felt it was inevitable he would slip. After only four steps, he missed his footing and was thrown off balance. He fell sideways against the banister with a scuffling and clattering that must have sounded suspicious to anyone nearby. The two boys froze.

No one came to investigate, so they were able to carry on down—very slowly in Edwin's case, although he had decided to push his hood halfway back. It was flapping against his face and irritating him.

At the bottom, they found themselves in the hallway that had no windows but four doors leading off it. It was dimly lit by the usual small lanthorne placed on a high shelf.

"What do you think we ought to do now?" Edwin asked. "Should we split up? If we're both caught, that's the end of everything. If only one of us gets caught, the other can... I don't know."

Lanthorne drew Edwin into the dark space under the stairs. "Why don't you hide here while I try to find Swarme?" he suggested. "You don't know him and I do. You can't see in the dark and I can. We'll come and collect you."

"Absolutely not. I should go first, because it's my fault we're here."

"Edwin, I know you're very brave, but you're being a bit silly too. What if you go up to someone and say hello, and it's not Swarme? You mustn't think you have to do all the dangerous things."

"All right. I accept, under protest." He had heard his father say this.

Lanthorne tiptoed back into the hallway and pointed to each of the doors in turn. "*Eena meena mango mo, catch a maggot, chew him so.*" So it was going to be the left-hand door.

"Good luck," said Edwin. "Call out in a loud voice if anything goes wrong."

Lanthorne listened at the door, opened it slightly and closed it again. He made a *Nothing doing* gesture and moved across to the opposite door. He listened again, opened the door, slipped inside and was gone. As he slipped in, hints of a particularly unpleasant smell slipped out.

Edwin resigned himself to an anxious wait. Minutes passed, and he could feel himself beginning to shake. *I'll give him just a bit more time.* He thrust his hands deep into his pockets to keep them still, and tried to think of the best thing that could be happening to Lanthorne... He had met Swarme coming out of the laundry room, carrying a pile of towels. The brothers hugged each other and said, "Great to see you again." Swarme turned out to be very clever and came up with an astounding plan that meant they wouldn't need Trunke's help any more. They would track down Auntie Necra, take back Mandoline, and Swarme would have a door home open and waiting.

Edwin ran through this story several times in his head, and still there was no sign of Lanthorne. He clenched his fists. It was time for *him* to do something now. Time for the hero to go into the telephone box and come out with all guns blazing. He took the lighter out of his pocket and flicked it on. The bright little flame made him feel better. If anyone threatened him, he would make sure he stood next to the most flammable thing he could find. There was also the penknife if he was backed into a corner.

Edwin approached the door, listened, opened it and slipped inside. It was a heavy door with padding around the edges which served to keep most of this unbeliev-able new smell from escaping. Once inside, he was pressed back against the door by the overwhelming odour of something undeniably rotten. This wasn't the rottenness of green bread or squishy apples; it was the very spirit of decay, clinging and almost liquid. It seemed totally wrong.

Yet another passage lay ahead, with doors off it. Sickened by the unidentifiable stink, Edwin set off along it.

He drew level with the first door. This also seemed more solidly built, but he could distinguish sounds behind it. Was there a party of some kind going on? He heard laughter and a cheer or two, which sounded quite ordinary and should have made him feel more at ease, but didn't. Nobody could have an ordinary party in rooms infected by this vile new smell.

Then things happened in a rush. There was the unmistakable sound of footsteps approaching the door, and the latch moved. At the same time, a figure entered the passage at its far end. Threats were approaching him from every direction. Instinct told Edwin to run and not let anything stand in his way. He charged down the passage, shouldering the figure, a man, into the wall and making him spill whatever he was carrying. Edwin rounded the corner and found himself in the kitchen of the inne.

12

A Dish of Horrors

For Edwin, kitchens were meant to be warm and bright. They smelt of roast dinners and rhubarb crumble and invited you to come in and linger.

Here, he wasn't even sure at first that it was a kitchen he'd run into, it was so bare and cheerless. There was a stone range, with a layer of undisturbed dust instead of a fire, and a large stone sink into which a crude tap was dripping. The smell was much, much stronger. Part of him wanted to stand still and gag at what he was breathing in, but his only concern had to be finding a place to hide from the person he'd just collided with. There were several doors that probably opened into larders but, remembering the face-punching shock when he came face to face with the rotting store of food in Jugge's kitchen, he didn't dare risk opening any of them.

He heard footsteps that were definitely coming in his direction. In the middle of the kitchen stood a chopping block on four solid legs. A large meat cleaver had been left on top of it and for a moment Edwin thought of picking this up and adopting a threatening pose. It was obviously too heavy for him and the saw lying beside it would be even less use. All he could do, in the end, was to stand behind the kitchen door and pull it further back against the wall. He put a hand in each of his pockets. In the right, his fingers found the penknife and in the left they took firm hold of the lighter.

Unable to see anything, Edwin listened carefully, breathing as softly as he could. The figure muttered something inaudible. Yes, it was definitely male. There was the sound of a door opening and such a gale of stink blew out of the larder, Edwin knew he would have passed out if he'd shut himself in there with it. It was the older brother, father and great-great-grandfather of the smell that had found its way into every corner this side of the heavy door, only now it had all sorts of disgusting extra strands added to it. It prodded the lining of Edwin's stomach with aggressive fingers, shouting *Be sick! Be sick!*

The larder door slammed shut, and Edwin heard a new set of sounds. Something was banged down, onto the chopping block probably, and something else was slopped about. There was rattling too. Food must be being prepared for dinner and the figure hummed as he went about it.

Edwin couldn't understand what was going on. Surely this was the person he had just knocked over, but the man seemed more intent on carrying on with his business than searching for the hooded boy who had run in here only moments before. Why didn't he look behind the door? An unsettling game was being played.

Vigorous chopping was followed by a few moments of sawing and then the figure gave a grunt as of a job well done.

He'll take it into that other room, and I'll be able to find a proper place to hide, Edwin thought. *Where does he think I've gone? And what's happened to Lanthorne?*

"You might as well come out," said the figure in a teasing voice. "And don't try running off."

Edwin stood his ground.

"Is he in the larder?" asked the figure. "I don't think so. Is he under the table? Can't possibly be. He must be behind the door, then. Let's be seeing you. Edwin."

Edwin slowly pushed the kitchen door shut. He was now in plain sight.

"Lovely to meet you, Edwin. I'm Swarme." He stepped towards Edwin with his hand outstretched. "On second thoughts, better not shake hands. Mine's covered in..."

Edwin's fingers relaxed their hold on the penknife and lighter.

"Where's Lanthorne?" he asked, finding his gaze drawn to what was on the chopping block behind Swarme, in a shallow wooden dish.

"He's safely outside. Which is where you're going. I was about to fetch you, when you came charging towards me. How lucky was that? Even luckier that no one else saw you."

Swarme was in his late teens, a lot taller than Lanthorne and he looked well-fed.

His cheeks would probably be considered chubby in this world of sunken faces, and there was a tinge of pink in his grey skin there. His nose, in contrast to his cheeks, was unnaturally thin, as if it were a temporary addition to his face until something more suitable could be found. His hair stuck out horizontally from each side of his head, like a pair of scrubbing brushes, and his eyes were bloodshot.

"Stop trying to peep behind me into the dish, Edwin. You won't like what you see. You knocked the first lot right out of my hands when you clattered into me, so I'm having to prepare it all over again. The customers are hungry and I'm in a hurry. I'll have to put you outside till I've finished my duties and we can work out what to do." He took a firm grip of Edwin's sleeve. "You really do shine, don't you? Much brighter than any of our lanthornes." He smiled, parting his dark lips and exposing a row of sharp grey teeth.

Edwin had always had an obstinate streak. As Swarme ushered him past the chopping block and did his best to conceal it, Edwin twisted his body so that he could look at it over his shoulder. He saw with horror that Swarme had been chopping and sawing human forearms, many weeks old and rotting, dividing them into equal portions. There was an assortment of hands piled up in the middle of the dish like chicken wings, their slender bones peeking through the corrupted skin.

And then Edwin was outside in the pitch darkness, not caring who heard him when he vomited nor where he sprayed it. Swarme was talking to him urgently and Lanthorne was there too, but Edwin wasn't capable of conversation. Eventually he dropped face-down on the ground, paying no attention to where he was or what he was lying on; all he wanted was for the past few minutes to be wiped from his memory for ever. He knew what he had seen and what it meant. He now understood the smell which had seemed so completely wrong when he first encountered it.

In this world they ate people, dead, long-decayed people.

Shudders of nausea ran through him again, and tears soaked into the coat sleeves in which he had buried his face. What was Auntie Necra planning for his sister? It wasn't a simple kidnapping any more.

In the end, Lanthorne's relentless prodding made Edwin take notice of the world around him again. The three of them were sitting on a patch of earth at the back of the inne. The building was only a few feet away from them, although the darkness hid it.

"Edwin, try to breathe slowly and thoughtfully," said Lanthorne. "That's what we say to people who go floppy and suspect they might have died. Edwin. Edwin. Edwin."

"Stop saying my name over and over again, Lanthorne. It's driving me mad!" As if seeing a dish of neatly arranged human forearms wasn't already enough to drive you into insanity.

"Well, if you're talking, you must be all right," said Swarme. "I've got to get back inside. They'll be wanting their..." The faint outline of a door appeared in the darkness as he re-entered the kitchen.

"*All right*," Swarme had said. Edwin was sure he would never be all right for the rest of his life, after what he had just witnessed.

"They're eating dead bodies," he said very slowly.

"Like the olden days," Lanthorne whispered. "Swarme says it's what they come here to do. They can't get away with it in Landarn."

A question needed to be asked.

"Do you?..." Edwin tensed, dreading the answer.

"Of course not!" said Lanthorne. "We're very different."

166

"Have you never, ever?"

There was a long silence.

"I don't think so. Perhaps when I was very small. I don't know."

"Do you mean, your mother?..."

"Auntie Necra might have tried to feed me a piece of... something, when I was little. She likes the Old Ways, but my mum doesn't at all. That's why they're always arguing. It's why Auntie Necra doesn't like me very much. I'm too modern. Isn't Swarme nice?"

"*Nice!* Lanthorne, your brother chops up dead people and serves them to other people in a dish. How can that be nice? He eats them too, doesn't he?"

"No!" shouted Lanthorne. He jumped up and moved away. "He doesn't. He never has. He's the food boy, that's all. He hates what they make him do. He wants to go home!"

"Why doesn't he go home, then?"

"Because Auntie Necra told the inne-keeper to stop anyone taking him back to Landarn. He really wants to be back home."

The last word was stretched out into a wail. It sounded as if Lanthorne couldn't cope with the idea of his brother being a cannibal. It would flatten most people.

Eventually there was a thump, as Lanthorne threw himself onto the ground some way from Edwin.

"Swarme doesn't seem to mind what he does," said Edwin. He wasn't prepared to drop the subject that easily. "A normal person would lose their mind if you asked them to saw up bits of a body."

"Auntie Necra tricked him into working here. She said he'd learn to be an inne-keeper and make his fortune."

Edwin snorted. "I'd have run away in the first minute. I'd have walked home barefoot, no matter how far it was."

"Don't talk like that, Edwin, please. Swarme's a good person, I promise. He says he can help us."

Edwin fought down all sorts of angry responses. Swarme was humming to himself when he chopped up the pile of forearms, and you didn't do that if you were sickened by your work. And what if Swarme planned to put him, or both of them, on the menu?

"Is he going to leave us out here all night?" he asked, willing to change the subject at last.

"We have to stay here until everyone goes to bed, and then Swarme's going to come up with a plan."

"That could take hours, and I'm getting cold."

"Edwin?"

"What?"

"Are we still friends?"

"I suppose so." At the moment, he couldn't bring himself to give a definite yes.

"Now you know why I didn't want to tell you about the olden days. If we mention them at school, they beat us with a stick."

I'm surprised they don't stab you and then serve you up for school lunch, Edwin thought savagely.

"A lot of families we know have changed their names," Lanthorne continued.

"Why?"

"Because they think names like Ghules and Grewsumme and Skellingtone give the wrong impression."

"What's wrong with Ghules?"

"Haven't you ever had Ghules in your world?"

Edwin thought hard for a moment, then the penny dropped. "Our word is 'ghouls', not Ghules. *Gools*, not *Gyules*. G, H, O, U, L, S. You get them in horror stories. They feed on..." English was one of Edwin's best subjects at school, so how could he have not noticed the significance of Lanthorne's name? The Ghules family's ancestors had once been ghouls, and now they were determined to kick the habit, like a family of smokers turning to peppermints instead. "Why didn't your family change their name, then?" he asked.

"My dad says names are unimportant, but I'm going to call myself something different when I'm older."

"Like what?"

"Oh, I don't know. Edwinhelper?"

"Or Shinerliker?"

They tried to laugh, but it was difficult.

"Jugge says one of the reasons people in your Shiner world closed the doors is because they didn't like people from our world coming through to practise the Old Ways."

"You can hardly blame them," said Edwin. "I really am getting very cold. Do you think there's any chance of the guests having an early night?"

"Swarme'll come for us as soon as he can."

They had no choice but to hunker down in their coats and wait. Edwin was aware of an unpleasant dampness settling on them, and the muscles of his legs were stiffening and becoming increasingly sore. He kept the backpack close to him, with his right arm through one of the straps. Its contents were all he had in this world to help him recapture Mandoline and keep her safe until they got back home. He dreaded losing it.

Edwin tried to empty his mind of thoughts, hoping this would make the time pass. One thought simply wouldn't go away: the meat dish Swarme had been using was exactly the right size for a baby, and the more Edwin told himself not to think about this, the more a picture of Mandoline—shiny and wriggling in the dish—fixed itself in his mind's eye.

It wasn't long before he was crying, noisily and continuously. Lanthorne was tactful and said nothing.

13

Regrouping

Edwin was so cold, despite wearing the anorak under his coat. He was sure frost must be forming all over him. The night dragged on and on, and then suddenly there was a change, a noise he couldn't identify, perhaps scratching or sniffing. These weren't sounds Lanthorne was likely to make. Someone or something must be close by. Twigs snapped and there was a long grunt, as if whatever it was was trying to force its way through a small space.

"Did you hear that?" Edwin whispered, struggling to his feet. His sense of direction didn't work at all in the darkness, which made the situation worse. His hands, despite being inside gloves, were now too cold for him to grasp the penknife or lighter.

"Keep your face hidden, Edwin," said Lanthorne. "Don't shine at it, whatever you do."

They stood very close to each other.

"What do you think it is?"

"I don't know. It's trying to get through the hedge."

"I hope it's a thick hedge. Does it know we're here?"

Of course it did. They could hear the creature's eagerness to reach them in every sound it made. A succession of loud snaps told them it would soon succeed.

"Inside. NOW!" said Edwin.

Lanthorne grabbed his hand and pulled him along. The back wall of the building was only feet away and Edwin banged into it in his night-blindness.

"I can't find the door handle," Lanthorne cried out.

"Yes you can!"

"It hasn't got a handle on the outside. Swarme must carry it about with him."

Edwin felt his way to the door and then started kicking and banging for all he was worth.

Lanthorne joined in, shouting, "Swarme! Swarme!"

With the sounds in the hedge getting more frantic all the time, who cared who opened the door? It was most likely to be Swarme, in any case; it might even be Trunke, who would have recognized their voices.

"Idiots!" Swarme hissed. "I was just coming to get you."

The boys knocked past him into the safety of the kitchen. Swarme slammed the door shut.

"I told you not to make a noise."

"There's something out there!" Edwin shouted.

The one good thing about being so cold was that his sense of smell seemed to have shrunk. He didn't feel so sickened when he breathed in. He noticed that the chopping block was bare and the meat cleaver and saw had been tidied away.

All three of them jumped as the "something" threw itself heavily against the kitchen door, scratched it a couple of times and then apparently went away. The noise made Lanthorne squeal and clutch his brother, who pushed him off.

"That happens all the time," Swarme said. "I couldn't name half the things that are out there. The thorns on the hedge are poisonous, but they still keep coming. Looks as if I rescued you in the nick of time."

"It nearly got us," Edwin said angrily.

"I said I was already on my way!"

"Will everyone know we're here now?" Lanthorne asked in a frightened voice. He was imagining all the other guests converging on them, delighted at the prospect of an unripe midnight snack. "You'll protect us, won't you, Swarme?"

"I don't expect I'll need to. They'll have turned over and gone back to sleep. Everyone's used to cries in the night in a place like this. I'm more worried about your friend."

"Why me?" said Edwin, puzzled.

"Not you, Edwin. The other friend, Trunke."

"What about him?"

"There are things I need to tell you about Trunke," said Swarme. "He had nasty plans lined up for you, that's for sure."

This time both boys squealed.

"I'm going to hide you in my room, and then I need to deal with him. He's probably out on the prowl already. Come on."

Swarme hurried them down the passage outside the kitchen and through the heavy door. They slipped across the hallway, through a second door and down two passages, until Swarme arrived at the door of his own room, which he needed to unlock. Once inside, he lit a tiny lanthorne and told the boys to sit down on the simple bed.

"Trunke may have a plan, but I've got an even better plan," Swarme told them. "The two of you wait here until I've found Trunke and talked to him. When I've done that, I'll explain how you can get your sister back. You're in safe hands now."

As soon as his brother had left the room, Lanthorne said, "Aren't we lucky, finding Swarme? He's come up with a plan straight away." He was so excited by this picture of his brother as their hero that he couldn't sit still and bounced up and down on the bed energetically until Edwin put a hand on his shoulder to restrain him.

"He hasn't told us what the plan is yet," said Edwin.

"Whatever it is, we're going to do exactly what Swarme says," Lanthorne announced firmly. "No peeping outside." As if Edwin planned to do that. "You can go to sleep for a bit, if you like. I know it's the middle of the night, but I'm too excited."

"This room's like a prison cell," Edwin said. "No window, no personal things. Nothing's painted."

"That's because Swarme's being kept a prisoner against his will," Lanthorne told him. "Imagine what he's been through."

All Edwin's imagination could manage was to replay the sound of Swarme's gentle humming while he neatly chopped up dead people's arms.

"I need to rest for a bit," he said. "We seem to be doing everything in the middle of the night. I just..." He toppled sideways slowly enough for Lanthorne to slip the thin pillow beneath his head. Edwin was so exhausted that he didn't even notice he was still wearing his backpack.

Lanthorne patted Edwin affectionately on the knee and got up and perched on the edge of his brother's chair—the big brother he hadn't seen for years, and who had promised to be their saviour.

When the key turned in the lock, Lanthorne jumped off the chair as if he had been trespassing, and joined Edwin on the bed. It took several hard shakes before he could make Edwin open his eyes, let alone sit up.

Swarme looked very pleased with himself. He dropped onto his chair and surveyed his audience. "That Trunke's a crafty one," he said. "But he's not crafty enough to get past me."

Lanthorne gave Edwin a grey *I told you so* smile. Edwin tried to smile back. His tiredness made any facial expression a challenge.

"He'd heard the noise and was on his way to your room," Swarme told them, pausing to let them share the tension of the moment. "I caught up with him just as he reached the door."

Swarme lifted his hand as if he were going to open the door himself. Lanthorne gripped the edge of the bed with excitement, but Edwin frowned. He wanted more information and less performance.

"What did you say to Trunke?" Edwin asked.

"I said, 'I've put them back in their room without anyone noticing, and I don't think you should hang around up here.'"

"What did he say then?"

"He asked me why I was poking my nose into things that didn't concern me."

"He would say that," said Lanthorne. "He's rude and horrible. He stole Edwin's horlogge and all my money."

"I told him I was your brother and I'd caught you both trying to go outside."

"Did he believe you?" Edwin asked.

"Why shouldn't he believe me? It was the truth."

Not exactly the truth, thought Edwin. "Have you met Trunke before?" he asked.

"Oh yes. I know old Trunke quite well. He's a regular here. Brings people out from Landarn every few months."

Lanthorne gasped. "Do lots of people come here for?..."

"They call it the 'Special Menu'. Trunke's your man, if you want to taste it."

"He was in ever such a hurry to get his supper," said Edwin. "He must have been in that room with those people who were laughing about what they were doing." His face was suddenly more green than shiny. Swarme noticed the change and decided it was time to reveal details of his great plan.

"I've thought of a way to make us all very happy," he said. "You get your sister back and I get to go home. You two lads have given me the extra courage I needed."

Lanthorne glowed with pleasure, as much as a person with grey skin can be said to glow. Edwin was all attention.

"You've no idea how hard it's been for me, living in this terrible place for the past six months," Swarme said, closing his eyes at the painful memory.

"I guessed what it was like," burst out Lanthorne. "I told Edwin." He got up from the bed so he could stand as close as possible to his brother, his hand on Swarme's arm.

"I'm afraid to disobey the inne-keeper in case he, you know, does something nasty to me," said Swarme. "I don't want to end up being..."

Lanthorne brought his hand to his mouth in shock. Edwin still remembered the humming and said nothing.

"There aren't many places where the Old Ways live on. This is one of them," said Swarme. "When the word goes round that the inne-keeper's got his hands on some... stuff, they sneak out here from Landarn. I call them the Outlawes. I don't know what story they tell their families."

He put his hand on top of Lanthorne's.

"You know I only ran away with Auntie Necra because I needed an adventure. I didn't expect all this."

Tears began to trickle down Lanthorne's cheeks. "You see, Edwin," he said. "I told you. I kept telling you."

Edwin and Swarme exchanged a look.

"It seems as if your shiny friend still thinks bad things about me," Swarme said in a hurt voice. "I don't blame him at all. If I was in a strange world and someone had kidnapped my little brother, I wouldn't know who to trust. They set creatures on me last time I tried to run away. I could show you the scars." He made a move as if to lift up his shirt.

"No, don't!" said Lanthorne. "I'll get too upset."

"What was Trunke planning to do with us?" Edwin asked as pleasantly as he could. "I'll do anything to get my sister back. Thank you for helping."

"We need to deal with Trunke," said Swarme.

Edwin didn't like the sound of "dealing with" Trunke. He didn't want him to be next week's, or rather, next year's—Special Menu.

"He's in his room for now," continued Swarme, "but he's an Outlawe through and through. Who's to say he won't sneak out and lock you up or hand you over to the inne-keeper?"

"You'd stop him doing that," said Lanthorne confidently.

"Which is where my plan comes in. I go to his room and make sure he doesn't come out."

Edwin gasped. "You mean, kill him?"

"I mean that I loop a piece of rope round the door handle and tie it to a nail on the wall. It's what I do if we have guests who aren't interested in the Special Menu. They need to be kept away from the kitchen."

"Then what do we do?"

"Your shiny friend's very impatient, isn't he, Lanthorne? Are they all like that?"

"That's a really interesting story. Jugge says..." replied Lanthorne, who was obviously happy to sit around and tell it.

"Not now, Lanthorne!"

"Then we steal Trunke's hansomme," said Swarme dramatically. "Auntie Necra will have wanted to get to Morting as quickly as she could. She's got friends along the road. A quick stop with them to feed your baby sister and then off again. I expect I'm a better driver than the one she hired, so I promise you we'll be in Morting in no time. We find your sister, probably tie up Auntie Necra, and tell her what we think of her while we're doing it, and head back to Landarn before anyone can stop us."

It was a wonderful plan, Edwin had to admit it. If they stole Trunke's hansomme and set off now, they'd be in Morting hours earlier than planned, which would give Auntie Necra less time to... to do anything harmful to Mandoline.

"I like that plan," said Edwin. He stood up, put his gloves on and pulled his hood back over his head to show how eager he was to leave. He had managed to push his tiredness aside for the time being.

"Won't be a moment," said Swarme and left the room. True to his word, he was back in no time at all.

"Trunke's safe and secure for hours," he said. "No one will pay any attention if he calls out when it's still dark. I'm the best in the world for knots. I heard Trunke snoring away and I thought to myself, *Little do you know what's going to happen when you try to open your bedroom door tomorrow*."

"What *is* going to happen?" Lanthorne asked.

"Nothing at all," said Swarme, "because I'm..." He waited for one of the boys to finish his sentence.

"Because you're very good at knots," said Edwin. He pushed his hood back again and made sure Swarme could see him smile.

"Those white teeth," said Swarme. "How do you cope with them? Now, I don't need to pack because there's nothing I want to take with me except my winter coat."

"You can't bear to be reminded of your life here," Lanthorne added, as if he knew all about such things.

"Exactly so, little brother. Let's find that hansomme. It's quicker and safer if we go out by the front door. Besides, there are things you don't want to see out the back."

Edwin was absolutely not going to ask Swarme what he meant.

Swarme put on his winter coat, which was ankle-length and seemed to be little more than a tube of cloth as thick as a carpet with sleeves that stuck out at right angles. "It's not as smart as that coat of mine you're wearing, Edwin," he said. "I'm pleased to see how well my best coat suits you."

As Swarme opened the bedroom door, Edwin unexpectedly took off his gloves.

"What now?" Swarme asked.

Edwin sat back on the bed, slipped off his backpack and fiddled about inside it. "One last check to see

I haven't lost anything," he said. "Mandoline's a baby. She needs particular things." He found the pocket with the notepad and pen he always kept there.

Swarme and Lanthorne stood waiting for Edwin by the half-open door, their backs to him. He continued fiddling for a moment or two, with his head buried in his pack.

"Ready," he said at last.

They hurried along the couple of passages that led to the hallway, and were soon inside the main downstairs room of the inne, heading for the front door. Edwin sprang another surprise at this point by darting away. A single lanthorne had been left burning near the fireplace and he rushed over to it, more or less able to see where he was going. When he reached the fireplace, he took a folded piece of paper from his pocket and threw it as hard as he could up the chimney. "For Jugge in Landarn," he whispered and waited anxiously to see if his message fell back down. A distant clicking sound from somewhere high up in the chimney reassured him that it wouldn't. It was the same sound he had heard in the Beanery when he sent his first note to Lanthorne.

Swarme was reaching out for the bolts fastening the front door when Edwin darted away, and the note had already been posted by the time Swarme caught up with him beside the fireplace.

"What are you playing at, Edwin?" Swarme demanded. "This is the most dangerous place you'll ever visit in your life. We can't waste time with silly games."

"I was just destroying a piece of paper with my name on," Edwin lied. "I didn't want to leave any Shiner evidence."

A rush of cold air told them that Lanthorne was holding the front door open for them. Swarme grabbed Edwin's sleeve and marched him out of the inne. When he had shut the door quietly, he took some deep breaths and put his hands on Edwin's shoulders.

"Before I go a step further, I want to tell you something," Swarme said. "All this running off and giving me smart answers isn't helping anybody. It's putting all our lives at risk. If we don't get away NOW and they catch us, the inne-keeper will put you on a VERY special menu, I shouldn't wonder. Outlawes will come in their hundreds to get a helping. Tell him, Lanthorne."

Lanthorne put his arm through Edwin's. "Why are you being so naughty? Swarme's doing his complete best to help you."

"So we know where we stand?" Swarme insisted.

"Yes."

"I'll lead on, in that case."

They crept down the side of the inne, following a track just wide enough for a hansomme. It led to a group of small outbuildings. Edwin could see so little he kept his arm linked with Lanthorne's and allowed himself to be pulled wherever they needed to go.

From somewhere in the darkness, Swarme said, "If you start acting the fool now, I won't be able to help you. Nagges are very unpredictable."

"I understand."

"They like their sleep, but they also like a bargain."

Edwin had no idea what Swarme meant by this. What sort of bargain? They could hardly be about to sell the nagge something.

Lanthorne deposited Edwin next to the wall of one of the outbuildings and went to help his brother. Edwin had seen enough of the nagge's personality when they stopped on the way up from Landarn to realize it wasn't a good idea to blunder into one in the dark, so he kept very still. Footsteps moved backwards and forwards, with a lot of accompanying whispering. There was a brief, but exceptionally strong, smell of you-know-what, and this was followed by creaking and trundling noises as the hansomme was hauled out of its stable. Edwin felt the ground vibrate, as heavy hooves and then wheels moved past him.

"Come on," said Swarme. "I thought you were in a hurry."

"I can't move because I can't see," Edwin replied tetchily.

"I'll help you into the hansomme," Lanthorne said. "Swarme's got to feed the nagge. It won't take us otherwise."

Edwin clambered up the steps and flopped onto the passenger seat. Lanthorne joined him. Swarme's voice reached them from a point next to the nagge's head. It sounded as if he was having a conversation with an unco-operative child.

"Don't say I never give you what you want."

The creature snorted.

"Half now and half when we arrive. That's what we agreed."

More snorting of a grumbling kind.

When they broke their journey to the inne, Edwin had heard the nagge munching on thorn twigs. He realized at once that the sharp sound now cutting through the night wasn't one made by twigs or thorns being chomped. It was the sound of powerful teeth cracking bone. He winced. There were several more sharp cracks and then the sound of contented, breathy chewing. So he was about to embark on the most important journey of his life in a hansomme pulled by an animal that insisted on a nosebag filled with human body parts.

"That's all you're getting till we arrive," Swarme said.

The nagge stamped one of its feet and the hansomme shook.

"You heard what I said!" Then, in a more cajoling voice, Swarme added, "I've saved some really juicy bits for when we get to Morting.

"I'm locking you two in," he said, when he climbed into the driver's seat.

As Swarme closed the first flap, Edwin caught sight of a bag by his feet. As Lanthorne's brother had made a point of not bringing any luggage with him, the bag could only contain one thing—the nagge's next meal.

"Someone's bound to have heard the hansomme, so we need to get out of here before they try and stop us," said Swarme.

"Will they follow us?" Edwin asked.

"Once they see we've gone, they'll get back to what they came here for. And Trunke can whistle for a hansomme. Now stop wasting valuable time. It'll be a bumpy ride to start with."

Swarme chuckled at this thought as he banged the second flap across.

"He's so happy to get away from here," Lanthorne said. "Finding my brother was the best thing that could have happened to us."

Swarme was telling the truth when he warned them about the jolting. The nagge set off so fast the boys fell off the seat and the hansomme tilted alarmingly as it made its left turn from the inne track out onto the main road. Lanthorne laughed excitedly, and from

186

outside they heard a couple of shrill whoops of delight from Swarme. These would have woken up the sleepers in the inne, if nothing else did. Edwin prayed that he wasn't going to add hansomme-travel-sickness to his other troubles.

"This is going to be such fun," said Lanthorne. Edwin slumped into his corner, clutching the backpack. Yet another drive in the early hours of the morning meant he now had two nights' sleep to make up. He would be no help at all to Mandoline in his present state.

Edwin hadn't been asleep long when Lanthorne shook him awake to the sound of Swarme shouting angrily. The boys could also hear an assortment of excited animal noises.

The speed of the hansomme increased to a dangerous level and it rocked so much from side to side that Edwin was sure they were going to overturn and be badly injured. How many animals were there? It sounded like a whole pack. Then the commotion stopped as suddenly as it had begun.

Edwin was convinced Trunke and the inne-keeper had pursued them with dogs or other, weirder beasts. They were surely about to be taken prisoner. He put his hands in his pockets for the penknife and lighter. These wouldn't be much defence against two grown men who must have overpowered Swarme and possibly even killed him. There would now be three bodies on a bumper Special Menu. Edwin was so frightened he could taste sick in his mouth.

The flaps were thrown back and the boys cried out. Edwin was still fumbling with the penknife, but it was Swarme.

"A pair of wild *things*," he said. "They came up on us from behind. Don't know what they were; could only see their jaws. I tried to outrun them, but they were speedy little devils. I threw them half the nagge's supper, but they weren't interested. In the end, the good old nagge caught them both with its hooves. You may have heard the yelps. I quite enjoyed it, in a strange sort of way, but roll on morning."

Laughing, Swarme banged down the flaps. Edwin and Lanthorne managed to laugh too.

The attack had nearly made them crash, but at least Edwin had learnt there were a few creatures in this world who turned up their noses at chunks of long-dead human being. And in a grudging way he was beginning to like Swarme after all. Nobody else in this world had squared up to wild animals for him.

Despite his exhaustion, Edwin knew it would take him a while to calm down enough to sleep. A few questions had been unsettling him and now was as good a time as any to raise them.

"Do Outlawes murder people specially, or do they wait until people die to get their Special Menu?"

"Pardon?" Lanthorne had already started going "Wheee!" again each time they bounced over a pothole, and Edwin's question took him by surprise.

"Do Outlawes get impatient and murder people if they're feeling hungry?"

"I told you, the teachers beat us with a stick if we talk about the olden days at school."

"Don't pretend you haven't got any idea, Lanthorne, because I don't believe you!"

Edwin had raised his voice and could feel his whole body shaking. He needed to know exactly what sort of world he and Mandoline had been dragged into, and Lanthorne's evasions were more than he could take.

Lanthorne saw he couldn't get away with silence. "This is what I heard somewhere," he said quietly. "When people died and were put in their burial boxe, Outlawes might come along and steal the boxe, if it wasn't buried deep enough. They'd wait until the dead person was ripe enough and then they'd have the Special Menu."

Edwin was silent for a long time and Lanthorne didn't know if he was expected to say more.

"Sorry I shouted at you," Edwin said eventually. He was sickened by the possibilities that were racing through his head, bumping into each other and making new, equally terrifying scenarios. Mandoline was so tiny, no more than a snack for a few people. If Auntie Necra intended her for the Special Menu, she might be happy to wait for years until there was lots more of Mandoline to go round. And then what?

"I'm going to sleep now," he said. Asking the questions had only made him feel worse. Sleep without dreams was what his body needed and then he would have his full strength to take on Auntie Necra. It was good to have Swarme as an ally, because if Lanthorne's brother could kick aside attacking *things*, Auntie Necra wouldn't stand a chance.

Edwin spent the rest of the journey asleep, apart from a couple of toilet breaks. They had brought no food, but his body was too tired to complain.

Towards the end of the afternoon, when he was awake again and sort of refreshed, Lanthorne suddenly said, "Edwin we're slowing down," and slid onto the floor as they turned a sharp corner. "I think we're leaving the main road."

Edwin became alert at once. He sprang up and started to bang continuously on the flaps. Swarme was obliged to open up, because the nagge had begun to react to the noise.

"What?..." Swarme began to say but Edwin, backpack on, was already on the driver's seat next to him, making it very clear he had no intention of being shut away again. "You mustn't be seen," Swarme said. "Not out here. You're a Shiner, remember? You'll give the game away."

"Who cares?" Edwin shouted at him. "I need to see where we're going."

"Edwin, please." Lanthorne had followed him up onto the driver's seat.

"Be quiet! He may be your brother, but he's bloody well not mine."

If Swarme's rescue plan came to nothing and Edwin was forced to save Mandoline on his own, he simply *had* to know the lie of the land. The road back to Landarn was straightforward, but this minor road to Morting looked different. What if he had to adopt a plan B that required him to drive a hansomme himself?

"If you're going to ride at the front, then cover yourself up properly," Swarme told him.

Thoughts were tumbling over each other in Edwin's mind. He had never driven a go-kart, let alone a hansomme pulled by a creature from a horror film. He began to look closely at the way Swarme managed the nagge. *Threaten it, promise it a reward when we arrive, or just set fire to its tail*, he thought.

Lanthorne made himself comfortable, sitting between his best friend and his newly rediscovered brother. He tried not to upset Edwin by smiling too broadly, but very soon he was pointing out features and chattering away.

"Please don't talk to me, Lanthorne," Edwin said. "I need to concentrate."

The road to Morting twisted and turned, as if it were too shy to draw attention to itself—or, more likely, as if it didn't want the outside world to know what went on there. It was a narrow lane with forks and branches off it that Edwin found confusing and hard to remember. If he ever had to drive along it with Mandoline on his lap, he hoped it would be during the hours of daylight, and that Swarme was leaving wheel tracks clear enough for him to follow.

14

Out There

There were none of the high thorn hedges that had bordered the road on the first part of their journey. The ground here didn't seem to have enough energy or even interest to produce anything taller than a few feet. This didn't mean that Edwin was able to see for miles. The lane to Morting was squashed into the bottom of a dip for its entire length. Steep banks rose on either side, and only occasionally was there a gap which allowed him to see beyond the lane. What he glimpsed was as dismal and depressing as the objects close at hand. The forks in the road and the branches off it were no more than new folds in the ground that quickly turned corners and never let you see where they were heading.

Dark grey, pointed rocks jutted out of the lane-side banks at all heights like iron spikes, and if there were patches of grass they were always a desiccated grey and looked as if they could crumble away at any moment. Bushes resembling untidy bundles of barbed wire filled in much of the space between the rocks. Any bird wishing to nest in one of them would have been shredded if it tried to squeeze between the razor-sharp twigs.

Edwin had once spent a holiday on the edge of Dartmoor, a place he found wild, and always soggy underfoot, yet it filled him with energy. What he saw as the hansomme rolled along was the kind of Dartmoor that Mother Nature might have come up with after a day suffering from a migraine, the children out of control, the dinner turned to cinders in the oven and the dog being sick on the best rug. There were rocks and razor-twigged bushes wherever he looked. He couldn't understand how Lanthorne found so much to interest him.

During their holiday on Dartmoor, Edwin remembered, his mother had drawn him to the window one evening, saying, "Come and look at this, Ed." They looked out at the sunset over Tarlan Tor. Streaks of a red, so deep you thought it would bleed if you touched it, had begun to finger their way across the western horizon. The streaks ran into each other until, for a few moments, the sky was a sheet of bloody splendour.

Family memories. Affection. People who were sometimes annoying or annoyed, but never grey, and who never dreamt of doing that dreadful, unspeakable thing. Edwin's thoughts turned to how his parents must be feeling now. They had been without both of their children for three days—the baby kidnapped, and their son, who should have known better, making matters much worse by running off. He wished they knew how hard he was trying to get Mandoline back. These thoughts wouldn't help, though, and so he stared out at the countryside to clear his head. He tried his hardest to superimpose colour on it, but the utter greyness won each time, insisting on charcoal and ash instead of any kind of brightness.

"Heads right down, you two," said Swarme. "This is Morting."

No, this is the end of the world, Edwin thought. *And I'm here because I hated having a baby sister and I said so.*

Dusk dripped into the narrow lane and began to spread in a pool across the untidy village. Squinting from beneath his hood, Edwin took in Morting's main street. The houses were set at random angles, as if their builders weren't remotely bothered about neatness or planning. There were no front gardens, none of the little touches which suggest houses are cared for and not a single light in the windows.

The hansomme and its three passengers appeared to be the only source of life and sound for miles. Edwin had expected they would sneak into Morting, because they were planning a kidnap, but here they were, sauntering along and drawing attention to themselves. They might as well be blowing trumpets or letting off fireworks, for all the secretiveness they showed. Edwin was also becoming increasingly worried by Swarme's careless attitude. Their driver had even begun to hum softly to himself.

"Shouldn't we be sneaking in?" Edwin asked. "We don't want to warn Auntie Necra we're here." His intention was to take her by surprise, tie her up, kick her "right up the bumption", as his grandfather said, and then get away with Mandoline as fast as he could.

Swarme winked at him, a lopsided, grotesque wink that made it look as if his eye were about to pop out. "Clever old Swarme has everything under control," he said. "I'm so pleased with myself I could almost whistle. Auntie Necra will be sitting in her chair chattering to herself, with no idea at all of the surprise I'm bringing her."

Lanthorne looked nervously from side to side. "Swarme, I'm worried," he said.

"Shut up," said Swarme. "I've just told you. I'm enjoying the moment. You should enjoy it too. It's not every day something goes perfectly to plan."

"We've done it, Lanthorne," Edwin said. "Or almost done it. Swarme's got us here."

"I know he has," Lanthorne said proudly.

"Let's celebrate with some speed," said Swarme, laughing. "Hold on, 'cause here we go." He stung the nagge with his whip, drove them, hell for leather, to the end of the main street and then skilfully guided the hansomme through the gap in a thorn hedge, before coming to a halt in front of a square house which was already losing its edges in the falling darkness.

"Is this Auntie Necra's house?" Lanthorne asked.

"The very same. Now get down."

Edwin was happy to obey. They were three against one, because Swarme hadn't mentioned anyone else living with Auntie Necra. Swarme could hold her down, while Edwin tied her up. They would even let Lanthorne bite her if he really felt like it, because she had hurt him often enough in the past.

Swarme deftly slipped the nosebag of Special-Menu scraps over the nagge's head and then, taking a firm grip on Edwin and Lanthorne, one on each side of him, he walked them to the front door. He had to kick the door because he wasn't prepared to relax his hold on the boys. His fingers dug painfully into Edwin's arm.

The door opened a little way.

"Hello, Auntie. I've brought you a present."

Swarme's mocking words crushed Edwin's hopes to the size of grit.

15

So Here You Are

Swarme let go of Lanthorne and used both hands to keep Edwin's arms by his sides. He was much stronger than Edwin and no amount of wriggling and shouting could stop Edwin being pushed through the door of Auntie Necra's house and taken down a dark passage.

Very quickly, he found himself in a small, dark room with the door locked behind him. He fell onto the floor, sobbing at the hopelessness of his situation. Lanthorne was outside shouting. He told Edwin he was sorry. He called his brother names and he started crying too. He must have been pulled away, because his voice became fainter. A door slammed and there was silence. In that silence, Edwin heard the only sound in the world that could lift his spirits at that moment—a baby crying.

Edwin sat up and did his best to calm himself. Mandoline was alive and she needed him. Rolling around on the floor like a six-year-old who has been told, "No more sweets," wouldn't help her.

Swarme had led them into a trap and Lanthorne knew nothing about it. That was clear. Unfortunately, nothing else was. Edwin could feel panic setting in. He removed his backpack and took the lighter out of his pocket. He flicked it on for long enough to see what was in the room, but apart from a low stool and a small unlit lanthorne on a shelf, there was nothing. Perhaps Auntie Necra regularly took prisoners, and this was where she kept them. He couldn't make use of the lanthorne, because that would let them know he had the lighter and he couldn't risk losing it. All he could do was to sit down on the stool and wait.

They can't leave me in here for ever.

Yes they could. They could let me starve to death and invite all their friends in Morting for a share of Special Menu.

If I starved to death, there wouldn't be much left of me to eat. That means they won't leave me in here for ever.

Edwin needed to be prepared. He stood up and tried waving the stool about. It was certainly lighter than the meat cleaver he thought of using back at the inne, but it made an awkward weapon and he doubted whether he could wield it effectively. Still, it would feel very satisfying just trying to wallop the treacherous Swarme and the vile Auntie Necra with it.

They must have been reading Edwin's mind, because when they finally appeared, each was carrying a heavy stick as well as a lanthorne.

"Stand back against the wall, little boy," said Auntie Necra. Edwin had caught a glimpse of her when he escaped through Jugge's front door, but now he had time to look the woman up and down. Although her lanthorne threw an elongated shadow behind her, she was quite little, which surprised Edwin. He thought he remembered her as tall and spiky, the kind of wicked person who looms over her victims and is prone to mad cackles. The fact that she was shorter than he was strengthened his defiance. Just let her try leaving pinch marks on *his* arms, the way she did with Lanthorne, her own nephew.

Auntie Necra was wearing a long brown skirt with stockings and boots of the same colour, and a muddy-brown and shapeless cardigan. Edwin wasn't taken in for a second by her *silly old granny* outfit, but at least she wasn't decorated with bloodstains. Her face was the customary grey, her eyes and lips dark and her hair was vertical as well as unevenly cut. Everyone had hair like this, so it was either what Nature intended, or the country's only hairdresser was a madman.

Auntie Necra breathed in and prepared to say something, but Edwin got his insults in first.

"You arsing cow!" he yelled. "You're both arsing cows!"

He moved forward menacingly and the two sticks were immediately raised. Swarme and his auntie looked as if they knew how to use them.

"So sorry we didn't light the lanthorne for you," said Auntie Necra. There was an edge to her voice Edwin found very disturbing. It was like the sort of voice that might enjoy saying things like, "That must hurt a lot."

"He's a proper little Shiner, isn't he, Swarmie? Much brighter than the baby."

Edwin came out with more insults, expressions he was reluctant to use even at school.

"No supper for him, I think," said Auntie Necra, as if Edwin was the one who was in the wrong. "Shall we let him have a bed?"

"Not sure he deserves it, Auntie."

"Whatever you say."

Edwin dredged up the filthiest words he could remember and shouted them all several times. He was shocked at himself.

"Someone we know is going to have to learn to be much more polite," said Auntie Necra. "We'll see if he's a nicer boy in the morning."

"I hope he's not afraid of the pitch dark, Auntie," Swarme added.

They were so taken with their little jokes, they didn't think of confiscating Edwin's backpack or searching his pockets. They were still giggling as they left.

Edwin sat on the floor for a while and took stock. Auntie Necra and Swarme weren't likely to bother him until the morning, so he could safely light the lanthorne for a while and sort out a kind of bed for himself. If there were going to be fights tomorrow, he needed to catch up on more of his lost sleep.

He chose a spot as far away from the door as possible for his bed and had no option but to lie directly on the floor in his anorak, with his backpack as his pillow and his coat as his blanket. He ate his last two remaining cheese triangles, which meant there were none left for Mandoline if he had to feed her on the run.

A cold, hungry, uncomfortable and miserable night lay ahead, but he had heard Mandoline crying and that made up for a lot.

16

Auntie Necra

Edwin slept in lots of little bursts. He kept waking to find himself in uncomfortable positions, with his shoulder or knee aching from being in contact with the same spot on the stone floor for too long. In the middle of the night, he was embarrassed at having to wee in a corner of the room because he was so desperate.

The room turned out to have a small window which let in a dreary, underwater kind of light that told Edwin it was morning. When Swarme burst in, Edwin was so stiff that the older boy was obliged to wait for him to struggle to his feet.

"You've been busy, I see," said Swarme, looking sneeringly at the trickle of wee which had run halfway across the room.

"At least I don't eat people. You're disgusting. And your hair looks as if it's made of old scrubbing brushes."

So much for his resolution not to shout any more, in case it made them even nastier.

"You do love your rude words, don't you?" said Swarme. "You'd be a terrible influence on my little brother. That's if we ever let you talk to him again. But where you'll soon be going, that'll never happen."

Edwin flexed his legs and shook his arms. He was loose enough now to pick up the stool or try to strangle Swarme with the straps of his backpack.

"You're so shiny, I can see exactly what you're thinking," Swarme said. "Your face is a complete giveaway." He pushed the stool away from Edwin, with the stick he'd taken the precaution of bringing with him. He prodded the backpack.

"Leave that alone," said Edwin.

"Full of precious things, is it?"

"Dried milk for my sister. So keep your hands off."

"Necra wants a word. If you're really polite, she might even share some of her plans with you." Swarme tapped the side of his extraordinarily thin nose, which bent slightly with each tap. "Don't you just love plans?"

Edwin dreaded the idea of Auntie Necra's plans, and he wished he could take a fierce grip of Swarme's nose and twist it permanently out of shape, or right off. He forced himself to remain calm. The main thing was to check that Mandoline was safe and not starving or being kept somewhere filthy. He quickly put his coat on and picked up the backpack. Swarme directed him out of the room and through the house to the main living room, where Auntie Necra was waiting. There was no sign of Lanthorne. Edwin didn't make difficulties or swear, but Swarme felt the need to rap him on the head with his stick a few times, just to make a point.

"Here he is," said Auntie Necra. "Did you sleep well?"

Edwin refused to answer.

"What's the matter? Cook got your tongue?" Auntie Necra and Swarme shrieked with laughter.

"Give me back my sister."

"Do have a seat, dear. You'll tire yourself out."

Swarme used his stick to push Edwin onto a rickety chair, while Auntie Necra made herself comfortable on a crude piece of furniture draped with a couple of blankets. The state of the room shocked Edwin, but it obviously suited Auntie Necra and Swarme. Cobwebs hung everywhere, some so heavy with old dust they looked like strings of dirty washing. Dust balls littered the floor in place of a carpet and, fanned out around Auntie Necra's chair, were the plates from which she must have eaten meals before she went to stay with Lanthorne's family. The air in the room had a sharp, stale tang, and woven into it was the telltale signature of the Special Menu. Any baby left in that atmosphere wouldn't survive for long.

Edwin couldn't judge whether Auntie Necra had dressed up or down for him. She had on a long grey dress decorated with smears and a pair of non-matching slippers that were threadbare and down-at-heel. Around her shoulders was a square of grey blanket which served as a shawl but which could just as easily have been used to wipe a dirty floor. There was possibly a flower in her hair, but Edwin stopped looking at it when it appeared to move.

"Shall I bind him hand and foot, Auntie?"

"Only his hands for the moment, Swarmie."

Swarme took a length of thin rope and tied Edwin to his chair, taking great trouble with the knots. Edwin put up a slight struggle, but decided he would go along with whatever they planned. If he looked crushed and obedient, they might let him see Mandoline and check that she was all right.

"I've always dreamt of having a little Shiner in the house, and now I find myself with two," said Auntie Necra. "*You* won't be around for much longer, but I've got spectacular plans for my shiny little princess."

"Spec-tac-u-lar..." added Swarme, with the most gloating sneer Edwin could have imagined.

"In the short time before you leave us," Auntie Necra went on, "you might as well make yourself useful. I'd welcome your advice on feeding your sister."

Edwin hated to think what they had been feeding Mandoline up to now. How dare this evil old bag call Mandoline *hers*? To help him control the whirlwind of rage he felt surging inside, he drew in a deep breath of the smelly air.

"My mum's shown me how to prepare a baby's bottle," he lied, hoping the instructions on the tin of dried milk were clear. "Her bottle will need sterilizing." He was pretty sure this was true.

Auntie Necra snorted. "How any child can survive on that revolting, unripe stuff you force down their throats, I'll never understand."

"Re-vol-ting," put in Swarme. "She's going to love *real* food when the time comes."

Edwin refused to be thrown off course by Swarme's taunting. "I don't think the dried milk will last very long," he said. "I'll need to go home and fetch some more."

This was a daft thing to say, worse than daft. Edwin knew it at once. Swarme sniggered. He rapped Edwin on the back of the head with his stick. "There's only one place you're going, and it isn't home," he said. "Aren't I right, Auntie?"

The horrible pair shared a chuckle at Edwin's expense.

"Please don't kill me," he whispered.

Auntie Necra and Swarme looked extremely offended by this remark.

"What sort of people do you take us for?" asked Auntie Necra.

"How absolutely rude," said Swarme.

"You Shiners may go about murdering people all over the place, but *we're* different," said Auntie Necra.

Edwin relaxed a very small amount. "When you said I'd be gone soon, I thought you meant..."

"We've found someone to take you off our hands," said Auntie Necra, with obvious satisfaction. "And not before time. I never realized Shiner children were so intolerable. A thousand times worse than Lanthorne, and he's bad enough."

"Please let us go home."

Edwin's captors gave him a long, pitying look.

"Doesn't he say the stupidest things, Auntie?" said Swarme.

Auntie Necra wiped the back of her hand across her forehead, leaving a jagged grimy smudge. "We were sending messages up the chimney all night because of you," she told Edwin. "Poor Swarmie's a shadow of his former self, after all that effort."

"Good job," said Edwin. His mouth was filling with swear words anxious to burst out.

"A man is coming to collect you the day after tomorrow," Auntie Necra continued, in a tone that showed she was becoming bored with the conversation. "Soon you'll be over the hills and ever so far away. Thank goodness."

"Over ever so ever so many hills," Swarme took pleasure in adding.

"Can I take Mandoline with me?" At least that way he and his sister would be together.

"What an idea! She'd never survive the journey. Nor will you, with any luck. At least you'll come in useful afterwards."

"What about Mandoline?" Edwin couldn't control the trembling in his voice, and his eyes began to tingle.

"She has a wonderful future ahead of her," announced Auntie Necra, brightening up. "With my help, of course. You'll be very proud of your little sister, or you would be, if you were around to see it. She's going to be the Shiner princess of the Old Ways. People will flock here to see her."

"She'll bring a new beginning," said Swarme. "I'm thinking of marrying her one day, if I get used to the brightness."

So they were planning to turn his sister into a monster like them, a girl who ate unspeakable meals and who might even come to enjoy doing it. Edwin wanted to scream, swear and throw up, all at the same time.

"Lanthorne admired you. He worshipped you," he shouted at Swarme, who now looked blurred through a sudden rush of tears. "He'll hate you for ever if you do this to us."

For a moment, a very short moment only, Swarme's expression changed. Then the look of sheer nastiness spread over his face again.

Edwin tried to blink away his tears. His nose began to run into his mouth.

"In case you're interested," Auntie Necra said, "your new master, owner, is called Limbe, or perhaps it's Legge, I forget. He's thrilled to bits at the thought of getting an actual Shiner. He sent us two letters in beautiful handwriting on tiny pieces of leather."

"Pieces of skin," Swarme corrected her.

Edwin shook his head to dispel the tears that were stinging his eyes. A streamer of snot flew across his cheek and attached itself to his right ear. He made a number of rough grunting noises and lifted his head.

"Is that a special Shiner habit?" Auntie Necra asked with distaste.

Edwin managed to say, "Please may I see my sister?"

"What do you think, Swarmie?"

"I'm not sure. All those bad words he came out with last night. How do we know he's sorry for saying them?"

"I'm really sorry," Edwin mumbled.

"I'm really sorry, kind Auntie Necra and handsome young Swarme."

Edwin dutifully repeated the words.

Swarme was no better than a playground bully making his younger victim squirm, but Edwin didn't care how much he squirmed as long as the story ended with him carrying Mandoline through a door into their own world. He was crushed, but not as crushed as they thought or hoped. Defiance began to resurface through his misery. For the moment, he was able to contain it.

"I'm really *really* sorry for calling you those names. Mandoline probably needs feeding right now. Would you like me to show you how to prepare her milk?"

"Swarme, give the milk to Buckette," said Auntie Necra. "She's in the kitchen. Edwin can show her what to do."

Swarme shook the contents of Edwin's backpack onto the floor. He was obviously confused by what he saw. Edwin nodded at the items they needed.

"That's the dried milk. That's the bottle and that rubber thing goes on the end of it."

Swarme picked up the three named items and brushed everything else to one side with his foot.

"Don't kick them in the dirt," Edwin shouted. "That's her favourite squeaky toy, and you can't put the blanket on her if it's filthy. Are you trying to kill her?"

Auntie Necra thought for a moment. "Take them with you, Swarmie, and give them a bit of a dust. All the other rubbish stays where it is."

Edwin pushed down the sides of his mouth so that he looked suitably downcast, despite being allowed to help feed Mandoline. For all their smugness, they had no idea he still had a penknife and a lighter. Auntie Necra's main room seemed very flammable. There was bound to be enough fuel left in the lighter for him to be able to set fire to a few items she treasured, if he had the chance.

Another idea came to him.

"That's a very delicious kind of sweet you're nearly standing on," he said. "It's sort of ripe."

It was a tube of antiseptic ointment around which his mother had stuck her own label saying "Baby".

Swarme took the bait and picked up the tube.

"I'll enjoy eating this at my leisure," he said as he untied Edwin. "If it's good enough for baby, it's good enough for Swarme."

He led Edwin into the kitchen where, surprisingly, a decent fire had been lit. Sitting in front of the fire, and protecting herself from it with a large wooden tray, was Buckette. She reminded Edwin of a bundle of old clothes to which someone had carelessly attached a pair of bony hands and a wig.

Buckette was muttering to herself. As Edwin approached her, he realized that she was saying, "I hate these flames," over and over again. Milk was being warmed for Mandoline in a filthy, misshapen saucepan pushed into the edge of the fire. You wouldn't have wanted to boil giblets for your dog in it.

Mandoline lay in a basket on the kitchen table. She was wrapped in blankets that didn't appear to have been used for anything else and she was waving her arms contentedly.

"Hello, Mandoline." Edwin took one of her tiny hands between his finger and thumb. Tears blurred his vision once again. Mandoline was never one to let bygones be bygones, and she began to cry almost immediately.

"She doesn't like you," said Swarme.

"She blames me for all this," said Edwin. "Do stop crying, Mandoline. You could at least say hello."

He laid the blanket he had brought over her, and squeaked the little mouse.

The crying turned to gurgling and Mandoline stared at her brother, working out what she thought of his arrival. She reached up for her squeaky toy and threw it out of the basket as soon as Edwin handed it to her.

"You need lots of boiling water for babies," Edwin said.

"Put the baby in boiling water," said Buckette. She joined Edwin at the table.

"No. That's the way to cook them," he said severely.

"Cook the baby in boiling water," said Buckette. She understood the point now and sounded as if she liked it. Edwin saw that her face was only a third of the size of her hair and it was covered in wrinkles, giving it the appearance of an antique, grey walnut.

"The boiling water is to sterilize the bottle," said Edwin firmly.

"Really?" said Buckette without interest. She leant over Mandoline and gave her a little pinch. Edwin had no way of knowing if this was done with affection or if she was checking on the tenderness of a future meal.

"I hate all these flames. They're not natural."

"What have you been feeding her?" Edwin asked. He wasn't going to be sidetracked into a discussion about fire.

"Unripe cow's milk," said Buckette. "Ugh, nasty stuff. All white and runny." She screwed up her face and half of it disappeared.

"Did you warm the milk?"

"Of course I did. I kept burning my hand. Look, there."

She held out the thinnest wrist Edwin had ever seen. It was so mottled and grey he couldn't tell whether it was recently burnt or not.

"That's dreadful," he said. "Thank you for taking the trouble." He didn't dare think where they had found the unripe milk. "I've brought a brand-new tin of dried milk. We mix it with water, but you need to read the instructions very carefully."

Buckette let Edwin take charge of preparing Mandoline's bottle. She hated the fire and she hated being so close to a Shiner boy. Whatever he asked her to do, she held her wooden tray in front of her face to shield it from the fire's heat and the glare from his skin. Edwin had to keep asking her, "Can you see what I'm doing? I'm not radioactive." Swarme looked on, but wouldn't help.

Edwin found some cleaner pans and washed them as thoroughly as he could under the cold-water tap. The water itself didn't look too clean, but he set it to boil by the fire and rinsed the bottle and its teat several times. Buckette muttered and tutted from behind her tray all the while.

Eventually they had a bottle of warm milk that Edwin thought his mother would be proud of. He approached Mandoline with it, and she began to cry at once.

"Let me have it," said Buckette. Mandoline stopped crying.

"You're a horrible little cat," Edwin told his sister. "You don't deserve me. You're guzzling that bottle while I'm practically invisible from hunger."

Swarme had been ordered to keep an eye on Edwin, but preparing the bottle took so long he was now bored and staring out of the window in search of something more interesting. Edwin sidled up to him and asked, in a small and extremely polite voice, "May I have something to eat, please?"

Swarme turned his head slowly. "Not so cheeky now, are we?"

"I'm really, really hungry."

Swarme flicked his hand in the direction of one of the cupboards. "It's just your luck that Necra was putting stuff away to ripen for New Year. Well, don't stand there expecting me to serve you!"

What Edwin did expect was that Swarme was playing another trick on him and that whatever "stuff" was in the cupboard had been ripening there since the house was built. All the same, he opened the cupboard door and could hardly believe what he saw. There was a dish of apples, a loaf of bread with only a suggestion of blue and green on its crust, and a piece of cheese that had decided to go hard before it collapsed into mush. Edwin was still wondering how much of this treasure he could stuff into his pockets, when a knife was waved in front of his face.

"On second thoughts," said Swarme, "we can't have you half-inching all our New Year nibbles. Hold your hands out."

He gave Edwin three of the apples, then took one back, and used the knife to cut a thin slice of bread and a corner of the cheese.

"Thank you," Edwin said, but his voice was drowned out by the sound of Swarme slamming the cupboard door shut.

Swarme returned to staring out of the window and Edwin helped himself to a drink of water to wash down the bread and cheese. The apples were kept for later.

When Mandoline's bottle was empty, Buckette decided to burp her by shaking her vigorously from side to side like a dog with a toy. Mandoline didn't mind this, but Edwin did. He rushed over shouting, "Not like that! She'll come apart." He draped Mandoline over his shoulder and gave her back the lightest of taps. She started to complain at once. Buckette shrugged. As they were standing next to one another, Edwin took the opportunity to whisper to Buckette, "My sister shouldn't be here. Please help me take her home."

It was a miscalculation.

"Swarme, he's saying things he shouldn't. He wants me to help them get away."

In a flash, Swarme had Edwin's arm twisted behind his back and was marching him out of the kitchen to another room on the ground floor of the house. Auntie Necra seemed to have prison cells all over her home. This new one boasted a separate toilette room, complete with unspeakable bucket and rag, a low bed with two blankets and a small, high window without glass. She must have thought that dust and cobwebs were only for special people, because Edwin's cell was fairly clean.

The first thing Edwin did when he was left alone was to lie down on the bed out of sheer relief. Mandoline was alive and apparently taking her residence in this dreadful house in her stride. He had kept repeating the instructions on the dried milk so, even if Buckette couldn't read, she should be able to remember how to prepare a bottle. The milk would last a week, but he only had two days to manage their escape before the man called Limbe or Legge arrived to take him somewhere that sounded a hundred times worse than Morting.

17

Four Legs and Lots of Stones

Edwin was left alone for hours.

If they thought this would break his spirit, then they had another think coming. When he began to feel uncomfortably hungry again, he took the apples out of his pocket and ate them as slowly as possible, sucking every drop of juice from each bite. They tasted surprisingly sweet, with only a hint that they were about to turn into something much less palatable. When he had finished eating, he lay on the bed for a while, staring up at the window, which was more of a ventilation hole and too high to see out of. It was also too small for him to crawl through, even if he could reach it. Despairing thoughts weren't going to get the better of him, so he jumped up.

Check everything, he told himself. He windmilled his arms a few times to show any despairing thoughts how full of energy he was, though he actually wasn't. He checked the door first. It was so solid he couldn't even make it rattle. His investigation of the walls and floor told him it was pointless to think of tunnelling out with only a penknife. Finally he rushed over to the toilette-room door, begging to walk straight back into his own world. If that worked, he intended to leave the door ajar so he and his father—and as many neighbours, policemen and off-duty soldiers as they could muster—could pass back through with guns and explosives. They'd settle the problem of Auntie Necra and Swarme for good. He violently pulled the door open.

"Armpits!" he shouted at the stinky little cubbyhole and slammed the door. He immediately opened it again, in case the powers controlling the doors between the two worlds had been shamed into helping him. They hadn't. He stomped back to the bed, shouted "Armpits" and worse a few more times, then sat down with the blankets wrapped round him because it was so cold even with an anorak and a coat. All he could do was wait for something to happen.

The something that eventually happened was Swarme's voice outside the room saying, "Get away from the door."

"I'm sitting on the bed," Edwin shouted back, wishing he were skilled enough to flick the penknife across the room and deep into Swarme's heart.

The door opened slightly and the end of a thick stick appeared and was shaken about.

"I'm sitting on the bed doing a crossword," Edwin said.

The door opened enough to allow a large tray to appear, the items on it sliding about because Swarme was obliged to carry it with one hand. His left hand held the stick.

"Auntie doesn't want you to starve," Swarme said when he was fully inside the room and placing the tray on the floor. "Well, not till you're out of her house. She couldn't care less what happens to you then."

On the tray was a plate with more bread, cheese and apples from the New Year cupboard. There was also a jug of water, a cup and a small lanthorne which was already lit.

"Everything you could possibly need," said Swarme. "If it was up to me, I'd let you go hungry."

If it was up to me, Edwin thought, *I'd force-feed you unripe food till you begged for mercy. But I'd still carry on feeding you. Then you'd know how I feel.*

"Auntie told me to give you this." Swarme took hold of a shapeless object which was slung over his shoulder and which Edwin had barely noticed. "She said it would be awkward if we had to tell Limbe you'd frozen to death." He threw the object at Edwin's head. "It's not fair, her ordering me to give you my favourite jumper.

You've already got my best coat and a stupid thing of your own underneath it."

"Sorry if I've got your most favourite clothes," Edwin said. "I expect you miss them a lot."

Swarme looked at him malevolently. He tightened his grip on the stick and Edwin flinched.

"Enjoy the dark," said Swarme, knocking over the lanthorne. Its light was extinguished immediately. Swarme laughed loudly, slamming the door behind him.

"What have you done to Lanthorne?" Edwin shouted.

"Don't you worry about him," said Swarme very loudly from the other side of the door, so that his every word could be heard. "He's having the holiday of a life-time—good food, new hobbies. Just what a lad of his age needs. You couldn't ask for better, could you, Lantie?"

A little voice said, "I love it here, Swarme." It sounded minuscule through the thickness of the door.

Edwin nearly choked with laughter. Swarme did the worst impression of his brother imaginable. If Lanthorne really had gone over to their side, surely they would have made him tell Edwin in person. He was probably locked in a similar nasty little room else-where in the house... Every speculation seemed to lead to a despairing thought of some kind.

Edwin decided to put the jumper on the bed, between the two blankets. Then he ate all the food and drank the entire contents of the jug in one go. At home he would have moaned bitterly if his mother gave him the same food two or three meals running, but locked up as he was, he knew he had to be grateful for anything. He wondered why the unripe food in this world always consisted of apples, bread and cheese. How welcome a sausage roll or a plate of jam tarts would be!

While there was still a thin beam of light from the tiny window, Edwin made several more excursions through the door of the toilette room. He was disappointed each time. All he could do now was huddle under his blankets. Before he did so, he flicked on the lighter and relit the lanthorne, which he placed beside him. Darkness meant despairing thoughts, but he hoped the glow from the tiny lanthorne would give him the strength to make plans instead. Edwin lay on his back, willing brilliant escape plans to appear in his brain, fully formed.

As ever, worries about Mandoline jumped to the head of the queue, pushing his other considerations aside. Would Buckette feed her properly or end up dropping her in boiling water accidentally-on-purpose? Would tomorrow be the day they put some of the Special Menu in her milk? And despite Swarme's laughable attempt to impersonate his brother, would they eventually convert Lanthorne to the Old Ways?

Edwin also had dark thoughts about his own future. Even if Auntie Necra and Swarme were exaggerating about the sort of life he could expect with the man named Limbe, *how did he get his name*? Why would you be staring at a limb when your baby was born... unless that limb was on its own, detached from a body and probably laid out on a plate in front of you?

"I don't want that to happen to me," he whispered. "It's *not* going to happen. IT'S NOT GOING TO HAPPEN!"

He blew out the lanthorne, because its flame was evidence that he still had his lighter, and very soon he had slipped into an uneasy sleep.

The winter light trickling through the little window was so feeble that Edwin had no idea how far into the morning it was when Swarme shouted, "Get away from the door!"

"I'm on the bed," Edwin shouted back. "I'm so cold and stiff I can't move." He was actually standing as near to the door as he could without his voice giving away his position. He thought he caught the sound of a second voice, Auntie Necra presumably, unless Limbe had arrived early.

Edwin tightened his grip on the water jug hidden behind his back. He had been waiting for this moment ever since he woke up and hatched the idea. Did they really think he was going to sit there like a turkey at Christmas and let them do anything they liked?

The door opened a fraction and there was the usual wiggly business with the stick. Next came the wobbly tray and, finally, Edwin's target—Swarme. As soon as he had a clear view of Swarme's head, Edwin hurled the jug and then threw himself after it, penknife in hand.

Swarme's reactions were annoyingly swift. He upended the tray to make a shield, and the jug exploded against it. Not a single piece hit the intended target. The breakfast, on the other hand, sprayed all over him before scattering onto the floor. By the time Edwin himself arrived, Swarme had strengthened his hold on the tray and he was able to swat the younger boy viciously aside.

Edwin's forehead took a hard knock. He staggered and swayed and lost all the advantage of his surprise attack. Swarme swept him onto the bed and sat down heavily on top of him. The blow from the tray had knocked Edwin's penknife down into the baggy sleeve of his coat so it had escaped Swarme's notice. He wasn't able to use it as a weapon, however, because his arms were pinned to his sides.

"Shall I break something, Auntie?" Swarme asked. "Just one or two little bones. Please?"

The other voice Edwin had heard did indeed belong to Auntie Necra. She had backed away while the battle raged, but she now entered the room and looked angrily at the mess.

"Don't break anything, Swarmie," she said. "Limbe wouldn't like it. If you sell someone a toy, you can't very well hand it over in pieces."

She came and stood by Edwin's head, which was half buried in the mattress by the weight of Swarme's body.

"You've been a wicked boy," she said. "You've smashed my best crockery and your nice breakfast is all over the floor. Well you won't get any more. Good food isn't cheap, you know."

Edwin wasn't able to call her the names he wanted to.

Swarme bounced up and down a few times and jabbed Edwin painfully with his fist. "I'm soaked and I only put these clothes on this week."

Edwin made incoherent sounds into the mattress. Their tone was clear, even if the actual words were not.

"I'm going to fetch Buckette to clear up his outrageous mess," Auntie Necra announced. "Don't let him move an inch, Swarmie."

With the eye that wasn't buried in the mattress, Edwin was able to watch Buckette collect all the sharp fragments of pot he hoped he might be able to use against Limbe when the man came to collect him. All that remained on the floor was the unappetizing breakfast. Swarme made a point of treading on most of it when he finally got off Edwin and left. Edwin salvaged a single unsquashed apple which had rolled into a corner by the door of the toilette room. There was also a piece of bread which he thought he might be able to put in his mouth if he rubbed it on his sleeve about two hundred times. After that, there was nothing to do but scream swear words and burst into tears at intervals throughout the Dikembra day, which seemed endless as well as bitterly cold.

Another night fell, bringing with it an army of the most depressing thoughts yet and sharp hunger pains to accompany them. Edwin perked up for a few moments when he had the idea that if he made his face fantastically clean he might be too shiny for Limbe to bear. With no soap and only a trickle of discoloured water from the tap in the toilette room, he was forced to abandon the idea. If Swarme had anything to do with it, he expected he wouldn't even be allowed to say goodbye to Mandoline.

"Get away from the door!"

At first, Edwin thought the words must be in his head, part of the jumble swirling round every corner of his brain. When the door opened a fraction, admitting the flicker of a small lanthorne, he knew he had visitors. But why in the evening? What could they want with him now?

"Sit on the bed, so we can see you."

Dutifully, Edwin swung his feet over the edge of the bed and sat up, with the blanket around his shoulders. A spiky shadow shot across the floor.

"You're ever so popular all of a sudden," said Swarme. "Your friend wants to check on you."

"Lanthorne?" Edwin asked eagerly.

"Don't be ridiculous. Lanthorne's never been your friend. Good old Limbe's arrived unexpectedly early and wants to meet you right away."

"Did you say *eat me*?" Edwin asked faintly.

"I said *meet*, but it's the same difference." Swarme sniggered. "Necra's bringing him along. Get over here. And none of your answering back. Your new best friend Mister Limbe isn't in a good mood. Something bit a lump out of him on the way here."

"Good job. I hope it was poisonous."

"Better not talk like that to him," said Swarme. "He's in a *really* bad mood. Whatever it was, left a few holes in his leg." He prodded Edwin with his stick. "And don't think about running out, because I'd be delighted to stun you with this."

Edwin's ears picked up the sound of shuffling and wittering coming nearer. Someone was holding another lanthorne, because there was more light and more shadows, distorted, wavering ones. Auntie Necra and a man leaning heavily on a stick came into view behind Swarme.

"...a truly nasty child, so don't take any nonsense," Auntie Necra was saying.

There was more than nonsense in Edwin's mind as he tried to push past Swarme and do whatever damage he could to the man who had come to take him away from his own world for ever.

Swarme kept his promise and cracked Edwin neatly over the back of his head. Edwin dropped where he stood, feeling blurry but not unconscious.

Three pairs of tatty, smelly shoes planted themselves too close to Edwin's face. Their owners stared down at him dismissively. Edwin glared dizzily back. He made his eyes focus on the stranger, noting the grubby bandages which had been wound many times around his right leg below the knee. In places, blood was seeping through. Long, talon-like fingers grasped the top of the walking stick extremely tightly, witness to the pain pulsing through the man's wound. Limbe's face was narrow and a sickly grey, with tiny, fierce eyes and a mouth turned down so sharply it could never, ever have smiled.

"Not much of him, is there?" remarked Limbe. "You led me to expect more."

"Too much attitude, though," said Swarme. "I should know."

"He'll need to get used to hard work," said Limbe, wincing. "My wife can't put up with slackers. I've lost count of how many serving brats she's worn out."

Edwin tried to lash out with his foot, but Swarme knocked it back.

"What's wrong round here?" Limbe asked. "Is there something in the water? I'm set on by a fangy thing, right on your doorstep, and now this Shiner boy wants to have a go at me. He won't last five minutes if he carries on like that."

"Quite right," said Auntie Necra. "Do whatever you need."

"The sooner the better," added Swarme. "Those shiny eyes of his give me the creeps."

"Make 'em or bake 'em, that's our motto," said Limbe. "So he'll come in useful, one way or another."

"Exactly," said Auntie Necra. "It breaks my heart to think I treated him like a prince."

Edwin had heard enough. He brought his knees slowly up to his chest and then uncurled suddenly like a spring. His legs knocked Swarme backwards into Auntie Necra while he tried to use his upper body to attack the man who was planning to become his master. He got no further than Limbe's knees but at least he had the satisfaction of hearing Limbe cry out in pain before Swarme and Auntie Necra bundled him across the room and threw him onto the bed.

"I'll kill you all!" he shouted as the door was slammed shut on him.

"No, you won't," said Swarme through the door.

"What's going to happen first thing tomorrow morning is that Mister Limbe, who is now in a worse mood than ever, is going to harness up his nagge. At the same time, I'll be tying you up so tightly you'll hardly be able to breathe and then I'll drop you head-first in the back of his hansomme. We'll take our fond farewell and you'll be driven off to your new for-ever home, for ever in your case being extremely short."

Swarme sauntered off down the passage humming and accompanied by every swear word Edwin had ever heard.

A little later, as Edwin was sitting with his head in his hands letting the echoes of another scream of frustration die away, he heard a crash followed by a long scraping sound. It seemed to come from outside rather than inside. A small part of him hoped it might be the fangy thing which had bitten a chunk out of Limbe's leg. With any luck it would squeeze through the window and quickly put him out of his misery. Most of him hoped it *wasn't* the fangy thing, though, and he was frantically thinking of how he could block the window and stop it getting in. He had already lit the lanthorne. If the creature was afraid of flames, he had the lighter as well, and the very small blade of the penknife. He gathered up his blankets, rolled them into a ball and then dropped them back on the bed. He couldn't reach the window, so why was he bothering?

There was more noise from outside. Edwin imagined the fangy thing getting very excited, with the smell of a Shiner in its nostrils. The scraping sounds had to be made by claws.

"Edwin, it's me. I'm up a ladder."

Edwin felt his chest expand with relief. He sped across the room and stood beneath the window.

"Lanthorne, get me out of here! Limbe's taking me away in a few hours."

"I know. I've got the key. Be ready. See you later."

More scrabbling and scratching and then a sharp cry of pain followed by silence.

"Lanthorne!"

Still silence.

Be ready, Lanthorne had said. So all he needed to do was sit on the bed and wait. But what if Lanthorne's cry meant that the fangy thing had got him too?

"Edwin! Edwin!"

He had fallen back asleep as he waited, and it took two or three vigorous shakes from Lanthorne before he came to himself. It was still dark, still night-time. He picked up his lanthorne and jumped to his feet.

"Where are they keeping Mandoline?"

"In a little room next to Auntie Necra's bedroom. We'll need to be ever so quiet when we take her."

They headed off through the house, Lanthorne tip-toeing ahead in the faint glow of the light he carried. Edwin's own lanthorne had almost burnt down and he wasn't sure how much light he had left. As they moved carefully along, Edwin noticed that his friend appeared to be limping. So Swarme was brutal enough to injure his own brother.

"Did he hurt your leg?" Edwin asked.

"I fell off the ladder, but it's not that. My pockets are full of rocks. I have to walk like this to keep my trousers up."

The rocks were a good idea. They might be the only effective weapon the boys had.

"I'll unlock the back door first," Lanthorne said. "We might have to run outside very quickly when we've got your sister. I couldn't do it earlier, because I was afraid someone would feel the draught."

Edwin's hopes were unravelling. This was the plan B he had dreaded. Assuming they got away from Auntie Necra, Swarme and Limbe, once they were outside they needed to drag Trunke's hansomme out of the stable and persuade the nagge to undertake yet another night-time journey. The creature would probably drive a very hard bargain.

I'm not bribing it with a bag of Special Menu, Edwin told himself. *And I need to keep Mandoline well away from it.*

233

Lanthorne carefully unlocked the back door and wedged it open with a chair.

"Now we can run straight out if we have to," he said cheerfully.

The breeze which blew in refreshed the room but couldn't disperse the background smell of the Special Menu, which had seeped into the very fabric of the building. They had passed through pockets of it on their way from Edwin's cell.

As the back door was in the kitchen, Edwin was saved the trouble of looking for Mandoline's tin of dried milk and her bottle. They were right in front of him on Buckette's tray. Luckily his coat had pockets big enough to take them. Then Edwin looked around for something he could use to threaten Auntie Necra or anyone else who got in their way. The knife drawer was locked, so he had to be satisfied with a ladle that was hanging on the wall.

"You do know where to go, don't you?" he asked.

"I kept offering to do jobs, so they let me out sometimes. I know where most of the rooms are. Follow me and don't talk."

They set off again. Every second or third step, there was a clunk as Lanthorne's rocks banged together. From the way he was walking, you would have thought he was wearing half a rockery. Edwin swung the ladle experimentally. It was heavy and he liked the feel of the handle. He would have to drop it once they found Mandoline, but he was prepared to put it to good use if anyone tried to stop them before they reached her. He expected to encounter Auntie Necra, Limbe, Swarme and Buckette, but they didn't know who else might be staying there. Lanthorne couldn't possibly have learnt all the house's secrets.

The boys crept up a staircase and along a passage, until Lanthorne stopped in front of a nondescript door. His collection of rocks clunked together again and Edwin accidentally let the ladle swing against the wall. It gave out a clear ringing sound which he made worse by trying to smother it and then banging the ladle against the wall a second time.

They would need to be very speedy.

"Hadn't we better leave the lanthornes out here?" Edwin whispered.

"I think we'll need them. I haven't been inside. I only know what Buckette told me. I'm not exactly sure where to find your sister."

Edwin's hopes were dust in the air. He had practically beaten a gong to announce their arrival and now it turned out they had no idea where they were going, but standing there, dithering, wasted precious time.

He opened the door and they stepped inside.

They moved their lanthorne beams across the room, foot by foot.

Nothing. Nothing. Nothing. The edge of a table. A basket on the table... Mandoline's sleeping basket. They had found her!

As the boys stepped across the room to retrieve the baby, there was a disturbance in the half of the room which hadn't been illuminated. If they had looked there first, they would have seen a bed and a figure climbing out of it. With a shriek, Buckette hurled herself at Lanthorne, the nearest target.

For someone who still needed to work hard on his tennis smash, Edwin showed the timing of a champion. He brought the ladle down as hard as he could on Buckette's head. She was knocked unconscious in mid-hurl, and crashed onto the floor on the far side of Lanthorne. Her takeoff speed had been so great that she slid right across the floor when she landed, and came to rest in a disordered bundle by the wall.

Edwin put down the ladle and his lanthorne, and leant over Mandoline's basket. There was no way Auntie Necra could have failed to hear the commotion, unless she were blind-drunk or dead. All the same, Edwin hoped Mandoline would behave herself and not struggle or cry when he picked her up.

"It's me. It's Edwin," he said. "You're going to be a good girl, Mandoline, aren't you, because I'm taking you home."

He was sure she'd recognize his voice and be calmed by his reassuring tone.

Mandoline had awoken to quick-moving lights and shadows, to figures appearing and disappearing, to loud noises and her basket shaking, so she did what any self-respecting baby would do in such circumstances—she took a very deep breath and screamed blue murder.

Edwin took Mandoline out of the basket, wrapped her and her squeaky mouse securely in the blankets and headed for the door.

"Put her down!"

Auntie Necra emerged from her bedroom and was immediately struck in the middle of her forehead by one of Lanthorne's rocks. She fell backwards into the darkness.

"What's this!"

Swarme was entering from the passage.

"Missed," he scoffed, as Lanthorne's first rock sailed by his ear. "Argh!" The second had scored a direct hit on his nose. Swarme doubled over, clutching his face, which gave Edwin and Lanthorne the opportunity to push him out of the way and start along the passage.

Edwin was horrified at how slowly he was obliged to move. He had never tried running with a wriggling baby before and it couldn't be done safely in the dark. Lanthorne led the way with his light and kept urging Edwin to hurry, because the two victims of the rock attack had already cleared their heads and come out of Mandoline's bedroom in pursuit.

In order to increase his speed, Lanthorne was shedding rocks as he moved along. Their pursuers were barefoot, so they might trip on them.

The boys were the full length of the passage ahead of their two pursuers when another bedroom door opened and Limbe came out to see what was going on. The look on his face showed that he summed up the situation immediately. He stretched out both arms to take hold of Edwin and the baby and discovered just how quickly a desperate Shiner boy can react. Edwin kicked Limbe's injured leg with enough force to send the ball a long way out of a football ground. Before Limbe even hit the floor, howling, Lanthorne had shied his two remaining large rocks very accurately at the man's head, knocking him senseless.

They were still in front of Necra and Swarme by the time they headed downstairs, but Edwin could feel Swarme's fingers touching the back of his coat. They entered the kitchen first, by a whisker, but were outflanked as Swarme and Auntie Necra raced around the other side of the table and got to the open back door first.

"Gotcha," said Swarme. There was a cut on his nose and blood was running into his mouth. "I think we'll have our little princess back, if you don't mind."

"Get the baby, Swarmie!" yelled Auntie Necra. "Then we'll eat the pair of them. I promised Buckette we'd have something tasty for Nollig dinner."

The large kitchen table divided the pursuers from the pursued. Edwin knew he couldn't fight while holding Mandoline. He would have to put her down on the table and then do whatever he could to overcome Auntie Necra. He'd leave Swarme to Lanthorne.

Swarme began to advance around one side of the table and Auntie Necra around the other. She was also cut and bleeding and very angry. The boys couldn't see any chance of escape. Edwin delayed putting Mandoline down as Lanthorne started to fire off the few small rocks he had left. At such close range, they were bound to find their targets, but he had little more than pebbles left now and Auntie Necra and Swarme made light of them.

Their advance seemed unstoppable, until a ferocious snarl erupted from the darkness just beyond the kitchen door. All four people froze in their tracks and turned to look in the direction of the sound. Two snarling heads appeared. They were attached to one body.

"Yes!" shouted Lanthorne. "I thought it was follow-ing us."

The enraged snarghe sank a set of teeth into each of Swarme's heels. These were warning nips and not meant to remove his feet, which the snarghe could have done if it had wanted to. It opened its two sets of jaws, releasing Swarme, who clambered onto the kitchen table, screaming. Auntie Necra joined him. Edwin was relieved he hadn't laid Mandoline down on the table, because Auntie Necra and Swarme were dancing all over it and they would have trampled his sister flat. The more they shrieked, the more this encouraged the snarghe to jump up and snarl at them.

"My snarghe's been following us all the time, Edwin. Swarme made the nagge kick it, so it remembers him. It must have sensed Limbe was up to no good too. They can work things out. Good boy."

One of the heads stopped snarling and fixed Lanthorne with an unfriendly stare.

"Good girl, too. Good boy and girl."

The two heads went back to snarling, as their single body jumped up to the height of the table top, making the figures on it scream each time the snarghe drew level with them.

Lanthorne turned to Auntie Necra. "I knew you'd be unkind to my snarghe when you found it in my room. Look where it's got you."

The relentless high-pitched sounds, screams, snarls and a baby howling, set off vibrations in every loose item in the kitchen. Edwin began to feel dizzy.

The snarghe hadn't enjoyed itself so much for a long time. It now moved on to its favourite tongue trick. Alternating neatly, the two heads unrolled and shot out their tongues, catching the dancing feet of the terror-stricken pair on the table. The heads could wrap their tongues around ankles, they could lash with them like whips and they could skin toes with great precision. All of these happened to Auntie Necra in the space of a few minutes.

The animal was the size of an overfed bulldog, with an impressive set of razor-like fangs, and mostly dull brown in colour. It looked as if its creator wasn't sure whether it was meant to terrify people or make them fall off their chairs laughing. Its two front feet had dangerous claws, but the rear pair were furry like a hare's and meant for running. It had fluffy black feathers on its shoulders and hedgehog quills of various lengths on its heads. The eyes in both heads worked independently of each other so it could look in four directions at once. Edwin noticed this and couldn't help staring as they zigzagged about. The effect was hypnotic, but he had to concentrate on getting Mandoline away.

"We have to go," he said. "Lanthorne, we *have* to go."

This was the first time he'd spoken, and at the sound of his voice, the body of the snarghe stopped jumping. The two heads focused on him alone and he thought they might be about to attack, just when there was the possibility of escape. He was on the verge of handing Mandoline up to Auntie Necra for safekeeping. Lanthorne nudged him.

"Talk to it, Edwin. It licked you in the cupboard and I think it's been following your smell because it loves you."

Edwin wasn't sure about that. He couldn't afford to waste time sweet-talking a monstrosity.

"Good snarghe. Good boy. Good girl," he said nervously.

The snarghe trotted over to him and sat down, with one of its paws resting on his left foot. He didn't dare pull it free.

A slight movement from Swarme, as he prepared to jump off the table, brought the creature snarling to life again.

"I'd stay there, if I were you. It's safer," Edwin said. "Good snarghe. Keep the nasty people on the table."

The room became much quieter. Mandoline was whining rather than howling and Auntie Necra and Swarme had started to whisper to each other. The snarghe moved back to the table and used a low growling sound to warn them not to try anything they might regret.

Swarme felt brave enough to say, "You won't get away, Shiner boy."

"Shut up," said Lanthorne. "Just shut up!"

He knelt down beside the snarghe, and pointed to his aunt and brother.

"Remember how much they hurt you. Keep them here for us, because Edwin and I need to take his baby sister home."

The two heads nodded.

"There's no point in talking to it. It's as stupid as you are," Auntie Necra called out. "Two heads, and less than half a brain in each."

She regretted her words at once. Both tongues shot out and completely skinned two more of her toes. Whimpering, she clung to Swarme. They were going to be stuck on top of that table for quite some time and they couldn't expect any help from Limbe or Buckette because both were out for the count.

The boys went outside and Lanthorne locked the back door and put the key in his pocket. Edwin rearranged Mandoline's blankets so that very little of her face was exposed to the biting chill of the night air. He was terrified she would turn to ice in his arms.

With Lanthorne carrying the light and leading the way, they headed for the stable. Edwin always knew they would never manage to roll out the hansomme and set it up for a journey. The attitude of the nagge confirmed this. As soon as they opened the stable door, there was an outburst of noise from the animal, an irritable *What are you doing disturbing my sleep, and if you think I'm going out at this time of night you must be mad* kind of noise.

"It almost sounded as if it said, 'Bugger off,'" said Edwin.

"It did."

The boys left the stable.

"Don't bother to shut the door," said Edwin. "Why should we be the only ones who die of cold?"

Mandoline's grizzling went up several levels and she pushed the blanket away from her face.

"Please try to be on my side, just this once," Edwin begged her. And then it began to snow, which meant he had to bury her even further in the blankets.

It wasn't the soft, brilliant white snow that we long for at Christmas and which rarely gets its timing right. That kind would have been pretty, even though it put paid to any hope of escape. This snow fell in giant, discoloured flakes, more like the ash from chimneys or a volcano. It was numbingly cold and melted into dirty streaks on Edwin's face. Simply standing there not knowing what to do put Mandoline in danger. He wasn't sure how long he could carry her. He hadn't eaten properly for days and his legs were feeling decidedly wobbly.

"Where can we go?" Edwin asked wretchedly. "We can't walk all the way back to Landarn."

Lanthorne's face didn't exactly brighten up, but he had an idea. "Let's knock on doors in the village and ask for help. Perhaps not everyone is like Auntie Necra."

"Perhaps they're worse."

"Perhaps they all hate her."

"Perhaps they're all having Special Menu parties at this moment. Anyway, it's late at night and nobody's going to be pleased if we start banging on their door and waking them up."

Edwin looked down at Mandoline's nose, the only part of her visible in the cocoon of blankets. This was the most difficult decision he had ever had to make. Their actual lives depended on it. "Give us a clue," he asked his sister. A small hand emerged.

"You see, she pointed!" shouted Lanthorne.

"She could just be letting me know she's very cross."

"Believe me, Edwin. She pointed towards the village. We might be welcomed with open arms."

"I suppose we might. All right. But if they turn nasty... I don't know."

"Follow me," said Lanthorne.

"We have to be very quick, before Mandoline's covered in a snow drift."

Even when you are as desperate as Edwin was, you still can't move quickly while holding a baby. They stumbled down the path in a jerky way that brought a lot of complaints from Mandoline. Although they had a lanthorne, Edwin twice lost his footing and thought his sister was going to fly out of his arms.

Once in the main street, they rushed to the first house and looked for the front door. As Lanthorne was about to knock, Edwin growled, "Don't!"

Lanthorne's hand remained poised in front of the door and then flopped to his side. "I can smell it too," he said. A recognizable stink, faint but certain, was escaping around the edges of the door.

"It's hopeless," Edwin said. "They're all at it." He gave Mandoline a little shake, to make sure she was still alive. Her piercing cry brought a stir of movement in the house and the boys ran off.

"Look," said Lanthorne. "There's a bright light up the hill. It's like a star. Nobody I know in Landarn would shine a light like that in their window."

"Why are they doing it?"

"It's a message. It's saying *I'm not like everyone else in Morting*. That's where we should go."

Edwin had to admit that the window, if it was a window, must be so bright for a reason. "It was hidden by bushes, at first," he said. "Now I can't stop looking at it."

"I think this is where Mandoline was really pointing," Lanthorne said. "Babies always know."

"It looks quite high up. Can you take us there?"

"I'll find the quickest way," said Lanthorne. "Come on."

18

Nearly Nollig

As they followed a zigzag path up the hill, the light continued to shine. All the while, the tainted snow fell relentlessly on them. Edwin was afraid it might be poisonous, and he slowed them down by stopping to brush Mandoline's blankets free of it. He knew that a scattering of flakes had reached her face. He was also concerned by her silence. If she was getting too cold to complain, that was a worrying sign.

"Prickly bush!" Lanthorne warned.

Edwin avoided it, slipped and fell backwards into another clump of sharp twigs. Several painful jabs told him that some of them had penetrated his coat and anorak.

"These thorns are everywhere," he said. "Can't you find a way through?"

Lanthorne was doing his best. Their tiny light revealed so little of their surroundings and they were constantly being caught out by the treacherous ground underfoot. He waved the lanthorne in arcs as wide as his diminutive arms could manage. "There's a wall of them," he said. "Wherever I take a step, I meet one. They're not meant to let people through."

"That's it then," said Edwin. "I hope whoever's shining that light is enjoying themselves. They're not different from the other people here. They're the worst of all. They wanted us to follow the light and get torn to bits by all these thorns. It being night-time and snowing probably makes it even funnier for them."

The little arcs of light continued flitting around the thorn bushes as Lanthorne tried to find a way through. Edwin could hear him muttering under his breath with increasing desperation.

"I can't go on or back or round," Edwin said. "I'm really, really tired. I've never had to carry something for so long."

The arcs of light were becoming frantic and Edwin could feel the strength in his legs and arms draining away, as if hopelessness had turned on a tap.

Suddenly Lanthorne called out, "Over here! Edwin, over here!"

Edwin wanted to respond, but his feet wouldn't move. A voice in his head was starting to say *You've done all you can. Time to give up and get it over with.* He could feel his knees sagging.

Then a lanthorne was held very close to his face, and he was being nudged forward.

"I think I've found a way in."

Edwin rallied. These were magic words, and he tightened his hold on Mandoline. Lanthorne had found a hidden gap behind one of the bushes, which turned out not to be a tricksy dead-end. There was a path that led to the front door of a small cottage which actually seemed to be painted a greyish yellow.

When they reached the front door, Edwin said, "No time to check. You bang on the door and we'll both shout."

There was no response to their noise at first, then from inside the house came a sound which was unexpected and which gave them heart. Someone was singing—a gentle, crooning sound that persisted despite their banging. It grew louder, as if the singer were determined to take no notice of them.

Edwin moved along the front of the cottage to the downstairs window they had seen lit up from the main street. A bright lanthorne had been placed between the curtain and the glass. He knocked sharply.

"Please let us in. I've got a baby." He hoped they didn't think he meant that he had brought something for them to eat, in the way that his parents took offerings of wine or chocolates when they were invited out to dinner. "It's a live baby." That wasn't any clearer.

The heavy curtain was moved aside a fraction, enough for the person inside to weigh up the boy standing outside, but not enough for the boy outside to see who had peeped at him.

Edwin returned to the front door where, all this time, Lanthorne had been shouting and banging for all he was worth.

The door opened and a voice said, "You'd better come in."

They needed no second invitation.

It wasn't exactly warm in the cramped hallway, but Edwin could tell at once that he was in a different kind of house altogether. The background smell was different for a start, almost sweet with a hint of the drainy smell he had noticed in Lanthorne's home. There wasn't a trace of Special Menu. He sniffed very hard to be sure of this.

The relief of getting out of the snow was so great, Edwin felt his legs buckle and he plonked himself down on the single chair, uninvited. He peeled away the wet outer layers of Mandoline's blankets.

Two large candles set on shelves around the bare hallway gave Edwin a clear view of who had invited them in. She was old and grey and her hair had the usual *I've just been given an electric shock* look, but her expression was kind and her smile revealed a set of teeth that were

250

severely off-white rather than grey. There were even hints of colour in her clothes, blue in her skirt and red in her blouse. The main colour was still grey, but the hints of brightness were exactly what Edwin needed.

"I'm Nanna Bowle," said the old woman. "I'm sorry I took so long answering. I thought you were the neighbours. They hate to see a Nollig lanthorne in the window or hear Nollig songs. That's why I sang them when you knocked. Now come inside properly. I've got a bit of a fire in the main room. It's a good thing I like to stay up late. Whatever were you thinking of, bringing a tiny baby out on a night like this?"

As they were led into the main room of the cottage, a room with four more candles and a number of half-comfortable chairs set around a thin brown square of carpet, Edwin said, "My name's Edwin and we're escaping from Lanthorne's Auntie Necra. She wants to turn my baby sister into a cannibal. Please help us."

"That Necra and her nasty Old Ways," said Nanna Bowle. "I hope you gave her a serious piece of your mind before you left her house."

"Better than that," said Lanthorne. "My snarghe was skinning her toes."

"A boy with a snarghe. There's a turn-up," said Nanna Bowle. "Now, you two sit down here and get the benefit of the fire. The first thing to do is make this baby comfortable."

251

Edwin adjusted Mandoline on his lap, so that he could take the tin of powdered milk and the bottle from his pockets.

"I'll add a few herbs to her milk to help her sleep."

"No!" Edwin said sharply. "My mother wouldn't like that."

He was the only person Mandoline could trust and he wasn't going to be tricked by an old grey lady into having his sister filled with strange herbs. For all he knew, they were designed to make her tender for Nanna Bowle's Nollig dinner.

"If you insist, dear. My, you do have a bright little face." She stretched out her hands to take Mandoline, but Edwin shook his head.

"There's no need for you to come too, dear," said Nanna Bowle. "I believe it's going to be a little messy."

"I'm not letting her out of my sight."

Nanna Bowle nodded and she and Edwin went into the kitchen where there was another small fire. Mandoline was cleaned, changed and fed, with Edwin looking on and wishing he didn't feel obliged to do so. His sister was as messy and smelly as he had been warned. She seemed grateful for the attention and didn't cry, until Edwin tried to amuse her with her squeaky mouse.

Nanna Bowle showed Edwin the herbs. They smelt as if they could only do you good, but he didn't see any point in taking chances and his response was still a firm no.

"If you've got some herbs for an itchy back, though, I wouldn't mind having them," he said. "I've been pricked by the thorns outside your house. They're not poisonous, are they?"

"Not exactly. But they can cause unsightly lumps. They're the best thing in the world for keeping annoying neighbours away. You should have told me straight away that they'd got you."

She took a pot of black grease from a shelf.

"Rub this where they've pricked you. Do it now and as soon as you get up in the morning, and then every day for as long as you need. The unsightly lumps only last a week or two in any case. Now, when I've tucked this baby up, we can think about some food for you boys. You'll also have to meet my grandson. He's sorting out his animal at the moment."

A nest was made for Mandoline in a basket lined with the softest blankets Edwin had come across in Lanthorne's world. She fell asleep as soon as she was laid in them, and Edwin could have cried with relief.

"We'll leave her in peace on the table, if that's allowable," said Nanna Bowle, "while I get the food. Go and sit with Lanthorne in the other room."

"I'm a Shiner, you know," Edwin told her. "I'm not from here and I can't eat ripe food."

"Can't eat, won't eat. It's all the same. I understand exactly who you are and where you've come from. Now you go and join your friend, and put some of that ointment on your back before you're dancing up and down with itches. And for Nollig's sake, take those wet coats off and dry them in front of the fire."

With surprising firmness, she pushed Edwin out of the kitchen. He found Lanthorne sitting well away from the fire in the main room and looking thoughtful.

"Let's dry our coats," Edwin said. "Mine's sopping."

"What if we have to leave again very suddenly?" Lanthorne asked.

"I'm not going anywhere till I've rubbed some of this stuff on my back. It's worse than itching powder." Edwin took off his coat and anorak and asked Lanthorne to hold his shirt up while he smeared handfuls of Nanna Bowle's grease over most of his back. The itching subsided very quickly.

"We can drape our coats over the backs of these chairs," he said. The fire was so half-hearted he imagined it would take at least a fortnight for them to dry. Lanthorne was still looking very thoughtful.

"What's the matter?" Edwin asked him.

"I know the lady's helped Mandoline and we're out of the snow, but why isn't she more surprised that you're a Shiner? She doesn't meet them every day."

Edwin had no chance to reply, because Nanna Bowle

appeared in the doorway carrying a tray. "Will apples and a bit of bread and cheese do?" she asked. "Don't worry," she looked at Lanthorne, "yours is lovely and ripe. I've warmed up two cups of tea. It's nice and fresh. I only made it two days ago."

Edwin took his food and sat as near to the fire as he could, trying not to see what was on Lanthorne's plate. He hadn't eaten properly for days. He was ravenous, and here he was with the same barely edible selection staring up at him. He turned to Nanna Bowle.

"I was wondering... I don't like to be rude," he said. "But whenever I've been given anything to eat here, it's always apples and bread and cheese."

"It's an invalid's meal," Nanna Bowle told him. "When we're a bit peaky and our stomachs can't take proper food, we're given the unripe things I've just given you. They're completely tasteless, but they settle the system."

Edwin gazed down at his plate. He tried hard to look grateful.

"It's just... Do you have an egg or baked beans?"

"You're very welcome to an egg, dear. I collected the eggs in June, so they're not completely ripe."

"That was six months ago."

"Eighteen months. It was June last year, now I come to think of it."

Edwin decided to make the most of his bread and cheese.

They had hardly begun their meal when there was the sound of a door being slammed shut and an outburst of crying from Mandoline, who was showing her annoyance at being woken up.

"That grandson of mine," said Nanna Bowle. "He can't do anything gently! You'll meet him in a minute. That'll be nice. I'll get the baby back to sleep, and then you can tell us your side of the story." She left the room.

"Do you think her grandson's our age, Edwin? We could make friends with him."

Edwin had no intention of staying around to find playmates for Mandoline and himself. He shrugged and concentrated on checking his piece of bread for signs of mould. *Your side of the story*, she had said. How could there be anybody else's side?

"They both looked exhausted," Nanna Bowle was saying as she re-entered the room.

"Serves them right," replied a gruff voice behind her.

Nanna Bowle and her grandson surveyed their guests.

"I've caught up with you at last." The grandson's yellow-blotched face was all too familiar to Edwin and Lanthorne. It was Trunke.

Edwin's jaw sagged, and what was left of his meal slid onto the floor. Lanthorne jumped up and ran to stand beside him.

Trunke looked very "out of countenance", as Edwin's great-grandmother used to say. A baleful glare from his sunken eyes took in both boys and let them know he held a grudge against them. Lanthorne half hid behind Edwin while Nanna Bowle gave a little, knowing nod.

For Edwin, it was a rerun of the emotions of betrayal he had experienced several times already in his search for his sister. "Mandoline!" he shouted, and rushed out of the room. It had suddenly occurred to him that the sound they'd heard might be that of the door closing after Auntie Necra left with his sister, while he was being craftily kept out of the way.

He returned a minute or two later to find that no one had moved an inch.

"She's still asleep on the table," he said.

"As we all knew she would be," said Nanna Bowle. "Why don't we all sit down? There are things we need to talk about."

"You knew who we were all the time," Edwin said, as soon as he had sat down.

"That's right, dear, but I thought if you saw Trunke as soon as you walked in, you'd be off into the snow again with that baby, like a jiggle after worms. So I told him to wait outside for a while, till I'd got you settled down. You do know that Trunke waited for days in that horrible inne until he could find another hansomme? He paid for it with his own money and drove all the way out to Morting to find you. How many other people would do that?"

Edwin refused to look impressed. For one thing, it wasn't Trunke's own money, and for another, he was wearing Edwin's watch.

"He's a good man, my Trunke is. That's why he's my favourite grandchild. He's not exactly cheerful, but who is these days? What possessed you to run away from him? And fancy stealing his hansomme, when he was taking such good care of you."

"Fancy eating people!" Edwin raised his voice at her. "He drives customers to that place for their Special Menu."

"Yes, I've told him it isn't nice," said Nanna Bowle, as if they were talking about Trunke biting his nails. "He doesn't partake himself. At least, not for years. Old habits die hard. I'm sure you find that in your world too. I've never tasted the Special Menu myself, and how many people can claim that?"

"I don't know what stories Swarme told you about me," Trunke interrupted, "but you were fools to listen to him. Look where it landed you! You could be home now, if you'd trusted me. As it is, I only arrived this afternoon."

"Now then, Trunkie, let's not dwell on past things," his grandmother told him. "They've been silly and ungrateful, because they're only young. I'm sure you've done things you're sorry for."

"And I'm sure I haven't," he said. "I'll get my own hansomme from Necra's tomorrow and then take them back to Landarn. I'm handing them over to Jugge as soon

258

as I get there. The hansomme I hired will have to stay here until I can make arrangements. They've caused difficulties for everyone."

"I said now then, Trunke. If we're just going to get cross, we should go to bed and sleep it off. We'll keep the arrangements until tomorrow. Although... I've got some lovely treats for Nollig Day. What about a titbit or two before you go to bed, Lanthorne?"

Lanthorne looked eagerly at Edwin. He was very tempted.

"Don't mind me," said Edwin.

"We'll go into the kitchen," Nanna Bowle told Lanthorne, "and Trunke can put down something for you to sleep on."

"I'm not their servant," Trunke said roughly.

"No, dear, but for the moment you're mine. Now be a good man and you shall have some Nollig treats too."

"Mandoline's sleeping next to me," Edwin announced. He went into the kitchen to fetch her, while Trunke collected their bedding. It consisted of a number of large, flat cushions and a pile of blankets, which he simply tossed onto the floor. He was about to douse the fire with a jug of water when Edwin stopped him.

"Nanna Bowle insisted my sister has to be kept warm all night, so we need the fire," he said.

Trunke grunted. He was obviously still keen to pour the water on the fire, but he wasn't prepared to disobey his grandmother. "I'm blowing out two of those candles, anyway," he said. "They're making my eyes sore."

"Thank you for coming after us," Edwin said. "What Swarme told us was very believable."

"And what I told you wasn't?"

Edwin had no answer to that, so he set about constructing beds for himself and Lanthorne. When Trunke left to enjoy the Nollig treats in the kitchen, Edwin put his sister on the floor next to him and said a very quiet, "Good night. Sleep tight." He would have kissed her if he thought he could get away with it.

Sometime later, Edwin heard Lanthorne slip into the second makeshift bed.

"Was the food good?" he asked.

"Delicious. We had..."

"No need to tell me." He didn't want a good night's sleep ruined.

Edwin slept so soundly that Lanthorne had to wake him the next morning. Mandoline's basket had already been whisked away, which annoyed him. He should be the one making decisions about where she went, not them. She would have been reassured, and friendlier, if he had been the one chatting to her when she woke up, and they had to go and spoil it by taking over. He dressed quickly and made his way to the kitchen. Lanthorne had already breakfasted but he kept Edwin company at the table.

Nanna Bowle said, "We've all eaten our fill. So has your sister. She seems to like it here."

Edwin made a non-committal noise. He was given a cup of the tea that was now three days old, a wizened apple and a piece of bread spread with butter that had an aftertaste.

"You won't like the jam, Edwin," Lanthorne warned him. He accepted the advice.

"Trunke's outside, having a word with his animal," Nanna Bowle told them. "He doesn't like the way it answers back. Now, I need to tidy up in here and you boys need to put your beds away. You don't mind if I keep Mandoline with me so I've got someone to talk to, do you?"

Edwin did mind, but he was gracious. He made a point of saying a few silly things to his sister—so that she remembered he was the most important person in her life at the moment, not a grey old lady—and then he accompanied Lanthorne back to the main room.

"Did you have a nice chat with Trunke over breakfast?" Edwin asked as he folded up his blankets.

"Trunke doesn't chat. He only shouts and threatens. He says he's going to do things to Swarme when he meets him again."

"I'll help him, in that case."

"Help Swarme?"

Edwin laughed. "No, help Trunke."

"Edwin, he's my brother."

"And he thought what Limbe was going to do to me was funny!"

They piled their bedding in a corner. Someone had added a couple of miserable pieces of wood to the fire while Edwin was asleep, and it was just about alive. Edwin looked around him.

"I know Nanna Bowle's doing her best," he said, "but I don't want to spend Christmas here."

"I wish you could spend Nollig with my family, Edwin. We'd have so much fun together."

"I can't do that. My parents need to have Mandoline and me home for Christmas. We'll eat a turkey straight out of the oven, not one we cooked in September."

Lanthorne chuckled. "You Shiners and your unripe food."

"Yes, we're a strange lot," said Edwin. "We scrape mould *off* our food. You spoon it on like chutney."

"I really have enjoyed meeting you, Edwin. I'll never have a better friend. I know we're going to be in touch always." He was clearly waiting for Edwin to say the same sort of thing back, and his face fell when Edwin remained silent. Edwin was afraid that if he said something like, "Yes, let's meet up again," no matter how insincere it was, the doors might be listening and spite-fully decide to make it happen.

"I've got a Nollig present for you," he said instead.

The disappointment which had threatened to make Lanthorne's face even greyer disappeared at once.

"A Nollig present! Where did you get it?"

"It isn't an *it*. I've actually got two. I've had them with me all the time, but I've only just realized I was meant to give them to you. One you'll like and the other you might not."

Edwin took his coat from the back of the chair, it was slightly drier now, and put a hand in each pocket. At first he couldn't feel anything. He pushed his hands into the pockets again. He couldn't believe they were both empty. Surely Trunke hadn't sneaked into the room during the night, gone through his pockets, found the penknife and lighter and stolen them? Edwin wanted to run straight into the kitchen and denounce Trunke to his doting grandmother. His fingers stabbed down into the pockets several more times.

"What's the matter, Edwin?"

"It's all right. For a moment I thought I'd lost them, but my coat was so wet the bottoms of the pockets had stuck together and buried them."

He took out the penknife and lighter.

"These are your Nollig presents. Happy Christmas and Nollig, Lanthorne. I wish I could wrap them in

Father Christmas paper and put them in a stocking, but I don't expect you go in for that. A penknife's always useful, and this," he ignited the lighter and made Lanthorne jump backwards, "well, you've seen it before. You never know, there may come a time when you need to set fire to something—the whole of Morting, for example."

"They must have cost your family so much money, Edwin," said Lanthorne, as if a lump of precious metal had been placed in his hand.

"They're just ordinary things that I want you to have. It's only friendship that makes them valuable."

"I'll try really hard to find something to set fire to," Lanthorne promised. "You'll be proud of me." He was still looking in awe at his two Nollig presents when Trunke banged into the room.

"Nanna wants you in the kitchen," Trunke said. "It's time to discuss things."

Lanthorne suddenly jerked his head up, as if there were something of interest directly behind Trunke. Trunke wasn't distracted and he didn't turn round. He watched Lanthorne slide Edwin's gifts into the pockets of his shorts, storing the information for later.

Here we go again, Edwin thought. It was into the kitchen, out of the kitchen, into the main room, out of the main room. Why couldn't he and Mandoline just leave, without having to hold a conference on it? He put

264

on his anorak, hoping it was a powerful enough hint that they shouldn't waste any time before setting off.

Nanna Bowle was sitting at the kitchen table with Mandoline, awake and interested, in her basket beside her.

"All the best decisions are made sitting around a table," said Nanna Bowle. "Take your seats, please."

Edwin and Lanthorne sat next to each other on one side of the table, facing Trunke. Edwin couldn't understand why Nanna Bowle was acting as if there was something to discuss. All that had to happen was for Trunke to retrieve his hansomme, tell Auntie Necra and Swarme where to get off, assuming they were still alive, and then they would head for Landarn and Jugge as fast as the nagge could be made to go. With no overnight stop at the inne serving Special Menu.

Edwin looked out of the window. Snow was still falling, drifts of grey covering everything in sight. Nothing sparkled. It turned the whole world into some region of hell where the fires have temporarily gone out.

Trunke twisted round in his seat and followed Edwin's gaze out of the window.

"We'll never get a hansomme through this snow," he said. "Mine or the hired one. So don't get your hopes up about leaving any time soon." He seemed to enjoy giving this disheartening news.

"But you said..." Edwin cried out.

"I never said we'd leave in weather like this. The snow will soon be up to the nagge's belly, and I promise you she's really nasty when she's uncomfortable. No, it's here we'll stay till the sun comes out. Could be ages."

You love rubbing it in, Edwin thought. He hated Trunke more than ever. "If we set off straight away, couldn't we beat the snow?"

"No," replied Trunke and Nanna Bowle in unison.

"What about finding a door in Morting? That would mean there'd be no need to travel at all." The panic in his voice was so pronounced it even communicated itself to Mandoline, who started to grizzle.

"I've never heard of anyone opening a door in Morting," said Nanna Bowle, "and I've lived here all my life. I'm going to finish my days here as well, so Lanthorne's Auntie Necra and her 'Old Timers' can put that in their toilette room and roll in it. Pardon my language."

Lanthorne sniggered, but stopped immediately when Edwin shot him a look.

"Couldn't I at least go round your house opening every door until I find one that lets us through? It worked when I did it in Jugge's house."

"You're welcome to try that, dear, but I don't expect it will do a bit of good," replied Nanna Bowle. "Morting's just not that sort of place. It'll be nice to have a house

266

full of people for Nollig. I haven't had that for years. I don't know where I'll find enough unripe food this late, though."

Nollig. *Christmas*. Edwin had lost track of how near to the 25th of December they were. If neither he nor Mandoline were at home on Christmas Day, his parents would have the worst time imaginable, staring at two piles of presents and thinking about their son and daughter who had disappeared.

There was a sound outside.

"There he is again," said Nanna Bowle. She got up and went over to the window.

"He and *she*," said Lanthorne. "It's both. It likes us to remember."

"They look very cold. Shall I let them in?"

"Yes please," said Lanthorne. "It's my snarghe, Edwin. It's followed us here."

That meant something had happened over at Auntie Necra's house. Possibly the snarghe had eaten everyone. Edwin wasn't too bothered if that was the case.

Nanna Bowle opened the back door and the snarghe rushed in. At the same time, something else rushed out. There was a streak of green. A *long* streak of green.

"There goes the jiggle," said Nanna Bowle. "We won't see him for the rest of the day. Not with a snarghe in the house."

Edwin could have done without the arrival of the snarghe and it bouncing around at his feet. It was an unwanted interruption when they needed to concentrate on finding him and Mandoline a door. Against his better judgement, he patted the nearest head. The second head shot him a hurt look so he had to pat that too.

"Perhaps they're hungry," he said.

The snarghe showed how much it agreed with this suggestion by putting out both tongues and swinging them backwards and forwards.

"I expect I can find it a stalk or two in the bucket," said Nanna Bowle. "They live on vegetables, you know, so, unless you've got a wooden nose, we'll need to go next door."

"A wooden nose?"

"Vegetables give them terrible wind. It's why they don't make very good pets."

These people ate food so ripe, the stink practically rendered you unconscious. If they found a snarghe smelly, Edwin was afraid Mandoline was in danger of being suffocated by one. He quickly gathered up her basket and returned to the fireside in the main room.

A tiny thought was beginning to grow in his mind, and he wondered whether everyone else would laugh at him and think him off his head if he suggested it. They sat in the main room for a while, with their idle chat turning more and more to how they liked to spend

Nollig. Even Trunke became a little sentimental. Edwin couldn't let their talk of returning home end just yet.

"Don't laugh when I say this," he began nervously. "When I wrote my first letter to Lanthorne, it was because I'd found a strange newspaper in an old house. It wasn't like one of our newspapers. I mean, the advertisements were really peculiar, magicky."

"I was feeling a bit lonely, so I put an advertisement for a pen-friend in *The Incredible Times*," said Lanthorne. "I never dreamt it would get through to Edwin's world."

"That's a newspaper for weirdos," said Trunke. "You should stay well clear of it."

Edwin couldn't believe what he was hearing. Trunke's own activities fitted every definition of weird you could possibly come up with!

"Isn't there a magic spell you can use to make a door?" Edwin asked.

The other three looked at him in horror.

"It's very rude indeed to say things like that," said Nanna Bowle stiffly. "I was just beginning to think you were a nice boy, despite your stealing Trunke's hansomme. I hope you're not accusing anyone here of casting spells."

Edwin couldn't understand their reaction.

"I'm going to check on the snarghe," said Nanna Bowle. "I may have to leave the kitchen door open for a bit."

"Now look what you've done," said Trunke, once his grandmother had left the room.

"What exactly have I done?"

"You suggested she might know spells," Lanthorne said. "That was ever so impolite, Edwin. We don't do spells nowadays. If we talk about them at school..."

"I know. Your teacher hits you with a stick. I can't understand it!"

"People want to be modern."

"This world doesn't make sense! *Nothing*'s worse than eating rotten dead bodies."

They sat in silence for a while, then Edwin got up and ran round the entire house, opening every door he could find, including the cupboards and the door of the toilette room.

He didn't dare go into the kitchen, where Nanna Bowle had shut herself. Nothing happened when he opened the doors except that dust flew out of the cupboards, and in Nanna Bowle's bedroom he caught sight of a gigantic pair of knickers draped over the end of the bed. This was the second time he'd run all over a stranger's house, but he couldn't think of anything else to do.

When he re-entered the main room, he gave the door a terrific slam behind him. The noise had the inevitable effect on Mandoline.

"It didn't work," he said when he sat down.

"I hope Nanna Bowle isn't going to ask us to leave," said Lanthorne. "We've nowhere to go."

"I'll go and talk to her," said Trunke. "She might need some persuading not to throw you out."

A whole hour later, Trunke and Nanna Bowle reappeared with very serious expressions on their faces. Edwin feared the worst. Perhaps he would need to take back the lighter from Lanthorne and threaten to set fire to Nanna Bowle's furniture if she showed him and Lanthorne the door. He imagined she might take pity on Mandoline.

"I'm willing to give it a try," said Nanna Bowle. "I should warn you, I'm more than a bit rusty."

Lanthorne's eyes were wide with shock. "A spell..." He gulped.

"It seems to be the only way. I've had a little practice on the snarghe. Not to find it a door, of course, but to see if I could still call up the power. I don't expect the creature will ever forgive me."

Tears filled Lanthorne's eyes. "Did you hurt it badly?" he asked very softly.

"No dear, though some spells have been known to make animals fall to pieces. This time the snarghe only rose up into the air and began to spin round so fast you wouldn't believe it."

"A good thing the back door was open," said Trunke.

"You should have seen the speed with which it flew out the door. Gone in a flash, like a..."

"Like a missile," said Edwin. He didn't want a spell that turned him or Mandoline into missiles.

"We need to sit round a table," said Trunke. "Come into the kitchen."

More backwards and forwards, thought Edwin. *This had better be the last time.*

He picked up Mandoline's basket, and he and Lanthorne followed Nanna Bowle and Trunke out of the room.

Both boys were taken aback by the odd smell when they entered the kitchen. It was metallic, with a hint of strawberries.

So that's the smell of magic, Edwin thought. He wondered whether he would ever come across it again.

Nanna Bowle drew the curtains and made them sit in particular places at the table, which she had already prepared. Edwin had to sit facing the window, because he wanted to move into a world of greater light, and Trunke was made to sit opposite him with his back to the window, because he was the most rooted in his own world. Mandoline's basket was on the floor a few feet from Edwin, near enough for him to take hold of it if he needed to, and far enough away so that nobody tripped over it.

"Lanthorne and I are halfway houses," Nanna Bowle said. "Free spirits, or whatever else you want to call us, so we sit at the sides."

She pointed to four small dishes she had placed on the table. "We have something to stand for each of the elements. That's earth. Trunke took it from the garden. Water from the tap, and the candle represents fire. All we need is air. Trunke, dear, could you put a coal from the fire in that empty dish? The smoke will do for air."

As Nanna Bowle was pointing across the table and giving her commentary, Edwin's chest began to rise and fall very quickly. Nanna Bowle took no notice, but Lanthorne was alarmed. Try as he might, Edwin couldn't banish the picture of the snarghe spinning round in the air like a catherine wheel, a catherine wheel that turned into a rocket. The giggles burst out of him as if they had a life of their own. He had only laughed like this once before, when he broke his arm and the doctor was about to set it. All through the stabs of pain and the tears, he had shrieked with hysterical laughter, and then he'd passed out in a dead faint.

"I know how you feel," said Nanna Bowle. "Magic used to get me like that, only with me it was uncontrollable hiccups. Now we need something from each of our worlds. A piece of bread from our world will do the trick nicely. Trunke, could you oblige, please? Everybody here uses bread to mop up their gravy, don't they?"

Edwin wondered what exactly she meant by "gravy". Certainly not the hot, recently cooked kind.

"We also need something from your Shiner world, Edwin. I don't expect you'd let me put your sister on the table?"

Edwin definitely wouldn't let her do that. He was only asking for a door to be opened for a moment. There was no way he was going to run the risk of Mandoline going up in flames or disappearing or taking off. He intercepted an unhappy look from Lanthorne, who was obviously thinking that he might have to forfeit the penknife or the lighter. Edwin gave a little shake of his head.

"I haven't got anything of my own in my pockets," he said. "But I do have a watch, a horlogge. Trunke's been keeping it safe for me." He looked hard at Trunke, who gave the most convincing *I don't know what you can possibly be talking about* look Edwin had ever seen.

"Come along, Trunkie," said Nanna Bowle. "You can have your horlogge back in a few minutes. Unless we all explode."

Trunke reluctantly took the watch off his wrist and laid it on the table, about six inches away from himself.

"I'd move it a bit further away, just to be on the safe side," his grandmother told him.

Mandoline lay quietly in her basket all this time. Edwin nodded to himself and bent down and lifted her up. He wrapped the blankets tightly round her, making sure that the squeaky mouse was inside. Then he sat

274

back down in his place, with Mandoline cradled on his lap. If anything good or bad happened, it would be better if it happened to them both and at the same time.

Nanna Bowle now began to work her spell. Her voice changed. It became deeper and echoey, and Edwin couldn't catch her exact words. They might not even have been in English.

Each wave of Nanna Bowle's hands and each intoned sentence changed the atmosphere in the kitchen a little more. The temperature dropped, and the light from the candle and the thread of smoke from the coal dish began to waver. Edwin could hear Lanthorne's teeth chattering. Something strange was definitely going on.

He held Mandoline more tightly against him, making her fidget because the new position was uncomfortable. *Please let a door burst open and bright light pour through it*, he wished. If that happened, he would be on his feet in an instant. He pushed his chair away from the table and raised himself six inches from the seat. No Olympic athlete could ever have started a race as fast as Edwin was determined to move towards the door when it opened.

Nanna Bowle clapped her hands and made them all jump. The candle flame went out and the smouldering coal on the plate flew across the room, barely missing Lanthorne's head. His squeal was drowned out by the sound of every door in the house bursting open and slamming shut as if closed by someone who was very angry.

In the silence that followed, everyone visibly sagged, hardly daring to breathe.

Is that it? Edwin thought. "Is there a door now?" he asked. He wasn't aware of one.

"Not right away, dear, but I might have set something in motion. Everyone, take a deep breath and put your hands flat on the table to ground yourselves."

Lanthorne's hands were shaking so much he couldn't stop them from slapping the table. Edwin relaxed his hold on Mandoline. So they weren't going home just yet.

Nanna Bowle stood up and handed Edwin's watch back to Trunke, who made a great show of refastening it on his wrist, avoiding Edwin's disappointed gaze. He wouldn't be giving it up again.

When the doors had slammed, Edwin was sure he'd heard screams mixed in with all the crashing. As Nanna Bowle drew back the curtains, they saw who was responsible for uttering them. Four faces were pressed against the glass, wide-eyed, panicky faces. Two of them were Auntie Necra and Swarme, but the others were strangers.

Edwin clutched Mandoline tightly again.

Nanna Bowle craned her neck to get a better view outside. "The snarghe won't let them move away," she said.

"Who are those other mad-looking people?" Edwin asked nervously.

"It's my mum and dad!" Lanthorne shouted with delight.

He rushed out of the kitchen and ordered the snarghe to release its prisoners. They scrambled into the safety of the kitchen and were disappointed and annoyed when Lanthorne allowed the snarghe to join them. It immediately herded Auntie Necra and Swarme into the furthest corner of the room and squatted in front of them to make sure they didn't move an inch. Auntie Necra had a normal boot on her left foot, but the boot on her right foot was huge and misshapen. Ends of rag hung over the top of it, and Edwin suspected that her damaged toes were now wrapped in the universe's grubbiest bandages.

Swarme got as far as saying "Mum...", but a yelp from each of the snarghe's heads silenced him at once.

Lanthorne hugged his parents and seemed not to care or not to have heard when Edwin said they were "mad-looking". Mad-looking they certainly were, their grey, pinched faces rising not quite vertically from the enormous coats they had both put on against the cold. Their hair was the wildest Edwin had yet seen but there was a kindness in their faces which made a change from almost everyone else Edwin had met in this world.

Nobody could be bothered to move out of the crowded kitchen and into the main room, because there was so much to say and so much catching up to do. Edwin felt ignored. Lanthorne's parents looked at him and Mandoline briefly, because they had never seen Shiners before, but they were really only interested in their two sons.

It appeared that Jugge had received Edwin's note sent via the chimney in the inne, and he had passed its contents on to Mr and Mrs Ghules. They had hired a hansomme so they could travel up to Morting to sort out Auntie Necra "not before time". Jugge had refused to come along with them.

Nanna Bowle set about preparing drinks, while Lanthorne's parents had their say. Because these were guests from Landarn, she produced cups of lukewarm tea with a suspicious scum on top which suggested it was even more ancient than the days-old brew Edwin had been drinking.

"Lanthorne, you shouldn't throw stones at your brother's face," said Mrs Ghules. "It'll spoil his looks."

"But, Mum, he's been serving up dead people, and eating them himself! They call it 'Special Menu'."

"It's just a phase. He's growing out of it already."

"Mum!"

"And call off that thing before it gets nasty."

Lanthorne motioned for the snarghe to move away from its captives. Reluctantly, it obeyed, but Nanna Bowle rewarded it with two cabbage stalks, one for each head.

Swarme smirked at Lanthorne. He was beginning to think he might come out of this better than he had expected. He touched his face and winced dramatically.

"It really, really hurts," he said.

What happened next was a surprise to everyone. Mr Ghules put his lips beside Swarme's left ear and bellowed, "Act your age!" He shouted so loudly that his son rose off the floor.

Mrs Ghules opened her mouth, ready for an outburst, but she was silenced with a look.

"More tea, anyone?" Nanna Bowle asked.

"I'm going next door," said Trunke.

"I'm ashamed of too many members of this family, you in particular, Necra," said Mr Ghules. "I'm ashamed of myself for not sorting you out earlier. All that ordering us about in our own home. As for the guests you have staying with you. Thank goodness that horrible man with the bad leg has cleared off home! It ought to be slaps all round. Except for our Lanthorne. He's the only one who's kept the family name out of the drain."

"My Swarme's not—"

Another fierce look from her husband cut off the end of Mrs Ghules's sentence.

"Our son started to go off course as soon as he joined that clubbe for youthe," said Mr Ghules, warming to his subject. "I could see the warning signs, but I wasn't paying proper attention. All those questions he used to

279

ask about the olden days and what they ate, and him and his friends daring each other to dig holes in the graveyard."

"All young people do that," interrupted his wife, who was determined to find something to say in support of her elder son. "Where else would they go to have fun?"

"And wanting his food riper than ripe," said Mr Ghules, without paying her any attention.

"You should blame Necra for leading him astray," said Mrs Ghules defensively.

"I most certainly do. She won't be welcome in our house ever again."

"*I* quite like unripe food, don't I, Edwin?" said Lanthorne, who was enjoying Swarme's comeuppance.

Edwin couldn't help thinking that it would be a while before Swarme felt in the mood to hum again.

The family turned in on itself like a doubles match in tennis, Mr Ghules and Lanthorne taking on Mrs Ghules and Swarme. Lanthorne enjoyed playing sharp little shots, incriminating comments meant to get Swarme into as much trouble as possible. His hero-worship of his brother was definitely a thing of the past. Auntie Necra shrank further into the corner from which she hadn't strayed since entering the kitchen. She looked like someone who knew she would have to watch her step in future.

Nanna Bowle caught Edwin's eye and pointed towards a very ordinary-looking cupboard door.

"That's the one," she mouthed.

Edwin showed that he understood.

He carefully skirted the quarrelling Ghules family and took a farewell look at his friend.

Lanthorne was glowing with pleasure at being with his family again; it was an extremely grey glow. Edwin felt in his pocket for the purse of coins he had planned to return to Jugge when they were back in Landarn looking for a door. He slipped it into Lanthorne's hand and nodded. Lanthorne nodded back and added a little poke to Edwin's arm. It was all over in a few seconds, and then Edwin was standing by the cupboard door to which Nanna Bowle had pointed.

With a final glance at Lanthorne, and making sure Mandoline was secure in the crook of his left arm, he took hold of the door knob.

Nanna Bowle had followed him. As soon as Edwin opened the cupboard door, she pushed him out of her world and back into his own. One moment he was in a kitchen, with its lingering smell of magic and the noise of a family in uproar, and then suddenly he wasn't.

As he was passing between the two worlds, Edwin felt something brush against his leg—a bucket or mop head—but he didn't look down. He was too happy gazing out into a bright December late afternoon.

It seemed an age since he'd last seen such real colours—an intense orange streaking the blue, with a hint of the first star. He breathed in the welcome vegetable smell of the allotment. So he had come through the shed door again, which meant he wasn't far from home. It was sometime near Christmas and appropriate for him to be standing with a baby in his arms. He shook Mandoline and she squawked. She was all right.

Some distance away, a couple of the frosted brussels sprouts plants began to shake violently. *Foxes*, Edwin thought. It was good to be able to work out what was going on. In Lanthorne's world it had been one hideous surprise after another.

As he threaded his way between the sections of the allotment, Edwin chattered to his sister.

"Just a short walk and then you'll be snug in your own little cot again," he said. "I expect you love that idea as much as I do, Mandy. You don't mind if I call you Mandy? You see, as I've saved you from a fate worse than anything you could imagine, I think we need to get on a different footing. Friends, not you getting me into trouble all the time. Okay?"

Mandoline winked up at him, or perhaps it was just her eye twitching as the first flake of snow settled on it. Edwin took it as a yes.

Something nuzzled his leg. Something nuzzled both legs, in fact. Looking down, he met the adoring gaze of two sets of crossed eyes. The bizarre heads which contained them were decorated with the remains of the recently savaged brussels sprouts.

When Edwin walked through his front door with the best Christmas present his parents would ever receive, they would be too overjoyed to bother him with questions at first. But sooner or later he was going to have to say, "Mum, Dad, I've got something to tell you. We were followed home by a snarghe."

QUALITATIVE INTERVIEWING